SCRAPPER JOHN
RENDEZVOUS AT SKULL MOUNTAIN

Other Avon Camelot Books by
Paul Bagdon
Featuring Scrapper John

SHOWDOWN AT BURNT ROCK
VALLEY OF THE SPOTTED HORSES

PAUL BAGDON is an ex-rodeo rider and horse trainer who has written a number of juvenile and western novels. He lives in Rochester, New York.

SCRAPPER JOHN

RENDEZVOUS AT SKULL MOUNTAIN

PAUL BAGDON

AN AVON CAMELOT BOOK

SCRAPPER JOHN: RENDEZVOUS AT SKULL MOUNTAIN is an original publication of Avon Books. This work has never before appeared in book form.

AVON BOOKS
A division of
The Hearst Corporation
1350 Avenue of the Americas
New York, New York 10019

CHAPTER ONE

Scrapper John Lewis grunted from the effort of holding his bow at full curve. It was early spring, 1887, but the weather was hot and sweat rolled down his forehead, chest, and back. The steel-bladed tip of his hunting arrow wavered slightly, ready for release at any second.

A magnificent buck, grazing at a clump of brush not far away, jerked his head up. The sun glinted on the polished points of his antlers. His eyes were suddenly alert and he sniffed the air. Scrapper John had a clear, straight sight line at the buck. A well-placed arrow could drop the animal where he stood.

The mountain boy's bow had been made for a man, and the strength required to bring it to its full curve and to hold it there while sighting for a shot was beyond most boys of fifteen. But Scrapper John had been raised in the Montana

Rockies by his father, Stone Pete Lewis. He had worked, ridden, and fought against the elements his entire life. His mother, a full-blooded Nez Perce Indian, had died of a fever before Scrapper John was five years old. His father had been killed by a grizzly bear less than a year ago, leaving John alone to fend for himself.

Unable to scent danger, the buck lowered his head back to the leafy scrub brush, an open target for a quick, easy kill. Scrapper John's fingers relaxed slightly on the arrow. His deep brown eyes flicked from the buck to the trunk of a massive oak tree on one side of the animal.

He took in a long, slow breath, held it for a heartbeat, and released his arrow. The razor-sharp cutting edge of the triangular head flashed across forty yards of sunlight. The arrow slammed home, buried itself an inch deep into the wood of the oak.

The buck was gone in a split second, leaping over bushes and fallen limbs. Scrapper John leaped to his feet and shouted after the fleeing animal.

"I could 'a got you, friend!" he bellowed. "You're plain lucky my pa taught me never to take an animal 'less there's no other way for me to stay alive. Your horns woulda been right nice over my front door, ol' pal!"

The mountain boy grinned as the deer disappeared into the heart of the forest. He turned. Musket, his dog, crouched close to the ground, waiting for a signal from his master before he stood. A short, almost silent whine escaped from the dog's throat. Three fat mosquitos had their stingers jammed into his snout.

"Sorry, Musket," Scrapper John laughed. "OK—git them bugs!" Musket was up before Scrapper John finished his words, slapping at his muzzle with a forepaw, growling in his throat.

"Hurry up there, boy," Scrapper John told his dog. "I got some prime trout bakin' on the coals back at the cabin, an' I ain't about to let them git all dried out while I watch you fight with bugs."

He crossed to the oak tree where his arrow was stuck in the trunk, and used both hands to pull it out. Then the boy and his dog strolled through the woods together, enjoying a cool breeze that had come up. Scrapper John practiced hunting daily. Although he made a game out of it, he knew it was a deadly serious business. Without his hunting skills, he'd have starved to death long ago.

Musket nudged at his master's hand with his nose, asking to be petted. Scrapper John stopped and tussled with the big dog, running his hands through thick, bronze-colored fur. Musket was the son of a wandering male timber wolf and a female collie. He was built like a wolf, lean and muscular, but his coat was the brassy orange of a collie. The wolf-dog had inherited the best traits of each of his parents, and he was completely devoted to Scrapper John.

Scrapper John's cabin rested on a small rise in a clearing at the end of a shallow valley. Stone Pete Lewis and his bride, Silent Fox, had built it years ago. Snowcapped peaks of mountains, as yet unnamed, towered in the distance beyond. The building consisted of one long room, unbroken by walls. A stone fireplace occupied most of the rear end of the structure. There was real glass in the windows along each side. Years ago, Stone Pete had traveled almost two weeks to buy the panes at the nearest town as a surprise for his new wife.

The cabin was tight and secure, the spaces between the skinned logs chocked with mud and clay. Over the years, the logs had aged to a darkish-tan color. Off to the side a three-sided shelter was large enough to stable three horses. Now, it held just one—Black Lightning, Scrapper John's black Appaloosa stallion with white spots on his rump.

Scrapper John knelt in front of the coals in the fireplace, and nudged some leaf-wrapped fillets of trout with a pointed stick. His thick, tousled hair fell over his eyes, and he brushed it back with his free hand. His skin, deeply tanned from a life outdoors, was not quite the amber shade of an Indian, but not quite light enough for the skin of a white man, either.

The leaves in which the fillets had been wrapped were singed almost all the way through, but the heat hadn't burned the fish. It was white and steaming hot, and the aroma

4

brought a rush of saliva to the boy's mouth. Musket drooled in anticipation of scraps.

Scrapper John moved away from the fireplace and sat cross-legged on a bearskin rug. Musket sat beside him, watching the boy chew mouthfuls of fish. He picked up a chunk and held it between his fingers.

"You got to catch this or you ain't gonna git it, fella," John told the dog. "I'm gonna count real slow-like to three an' then . . ."

Suddenly, a second voice boomed in the log cabin.

"I'd 'a had your hair swingin' from my belt an' the hide o' that wolf of yours tacked up on my cabin wall if I'd been a' enemy, Scrapper John Lewis! Didn't your pa teach you no better'n to set there talkin' to a dog like some dang-fool city kid?"

The voice was deep and hoarse and suggested laughter.

Scrapper John leaped to his feet, glancing quickly at the open window. "Eddie!" he roared happily. "Sweetwater Eddie!"

"That was my handle last time I checked," the huge mountain man outside the window grinned. "You're lookin' right fit, boy—for a half-wild pup, that is."

Scrapper John flew out the front door and threw himself at the man, locking him in a tight embrace. His hundred and fifty pounds of muscle rocked Sweetwater Eddie, making him fall back a step to keep his balance.

"Where'd you . . . ? What . . . it's great to see

5

you, Eddie! I . . ." Scrapper John stuttered, almost overcome at seeing his old friend.

"You'd best slow down before you bust your jaw, boy," Sweetwater Eddie laughed. "I figured you'd be happy to see me, but I didn't know you'd like to wet your britches. Come on—let's go inside so's I can git at that fish you was eatin'. I'm near starved. I been travelin' hard for all day, comin' here to fetch you."

Scrapper John rushed to put a handful of herbs into a pot to brew tea for his guest. He set the pewter pot directly on the coals to heat and turned to the mountain man, who was already gulping down the last bite of trout from Scrapper John's plate.

"I'm sure happy to see you, Eddie," the boy said. "What're you doin' out my way?"

Sweetwater Eddie belched loudly and wiped his mouth with the back of his hand. He was a bear of a man, tall, massively built, with muscles that bulged against the skin of his arms and shoulders. He was dressed in a shirt and trousers made from deer hide, with tall, soft-soled moccasins laced up the front with thongs of rawhide. His dark hair, much longer than Scrapper John's, had more than a few streaks of gray in it, and it was tangled into a greasy mess that hadn't been washed in quite some time. Eddie belched again, thunderously, picked a sliver of trout off his thick beard and popped it into his mouth.

"Ain't you got no manners, boy?" he rum-

6

bled. "Seems like you could find some more grub around here to offer a hungry guest."

Scrapper John hustled to the front of the cabin and fetched a gunnysack of salted and dried venison—deer jerky, as mountain men called it. "Tea'll be ready in a minute," he said. "You're the first person I've seen in a good long time, Eddie. I musta forgot some of my upbringin' because I ain't seen no one in so long."

"Kinda thought I'd find your Blackfoot pal Seeks The Far Sky here with you," Eddie said.

"Sky went back to his people jist after winter let up," Scrapper John answered. "He said he thought they needed him. I didn't argue none about it. I sure miss him, though."

"You and him covered some ground an' seen some times, didn't you, boy?"

"Yessir." John smiled. "We sure did. Me an' Sky are blood brothers. Our paths will cross again—you can bet on that. But you still ain't told me how come you're here."

"I was just gettin' around to that," Eddie said. "Remember how I promised Stone Pete I'd look after you 'fore he died?"

Scrapper John nodded.

"Well, I got to thinkin' that you ain't never been to a Rendezvous, an' that ain't right. Us mountain men gotta stick together. There's a sight fewer of us every year. One day, there won't be none at all. Anyways, I figured . . ."

"You come to take me to the Spring Rendezvous?" Scrapper John interrupted excitedly. "Really? You ain't kiddin' me or nothin'?"

Every spring the mountain men met for a major get-together after the long winter of hunting and trapping. They traded for supplies and brought each other up to date on happenings in the Rockies. But the main purpose of the Rendezvous was to celebrate the newly arrived good weather—a giant party that lasted for up to a week.

Without waiting for an answer from Sweetwater Eddie, Scrapper John howled with joy. "My pa was always tellin' me about them spring get-togethers," he said excitedly. "He said there was shootin' and wrestlin' contests, an' the best food in the whole world, an' lots of story-tellin' an' so forth. I been wantin' to go since I was a sprout. When do we . . ."

Sweetwater Eddie spoke between mouthfuls of jerky. "Seems to me like we're wastin' perfectly good daylight for travelin', boy. You about ready to go, or can't that Appaloosa of yours carry weight no more?"

"Black Lightning can carry weight, all right," Scrapper John laughed. "And he can carry it a lot faster than that mud-footed crowbait you come ridin' in on!"

"I guess maybe we'll git a chance to see about that, John. Now git movin' fore I ride off without you." Sweetwater Eddie stuffed another handful of jerky into his mouth and chewed contentedly. "Don't hurry none," he said. "I'll give you a minute or so."

A minute or so was all Scrapper John needed. He shut the cabin windows and raced to the shelter to saddle Black Lightning. They rode out of the valley less than a half hour after Eddie had startled his young friend by shouting in the window.

At first, the two horses danced and fought the reins, snorting at each other, while Musket darted around their legs. Sweetwater Eddie's horse was a tall chestnut stallion named Zinger that looked fresh and strong, even though he'd been ridden hard for a day. Black Lightning, his coat shining from a brushing by Scrapper John, pranced proudly, eyeing the other horse, challenging it with whinnies and snorts. Both riders handled their horses well, tapping at the bits with skilled hands on the reins, shifting their weight in their saddles to keep their mounts under control. But soon the horses calmed down enough to pace along together.

For the next three days, Sweetwater Eddie and Zinger set the pace and chose which way the riders travelled. Black Lightning, in superb condition, kept up stride for stride. Eddie used his army issue Colt to bring down quail and squirrels for meals. The man and boy traveled fast, not pushing their mounts but covering the miles rapidly.

The third morning out, Sweetwater Eddie told Scrapper John, "I figure we're 'bout half-way an' a bit better. See that rise yonder?" He pointed to a low hill not far off. "There's a range jist beyond it. When we git to the other side I'll know more 'bout where we are. I ain't rode this way in a slew of years."

The rise was more of a small mountain, and the climbing was treacherous. Melting snow undermined rocks and small boulders, which became dislodged and hurtled down at the riders and horses more and more frequently as they got closer to the top. The ground was slushy with water, and the horse's unshod hooves slipped as if they were on ice. Zinger, far more used to this terrain than Black Lightning, was fifty yards ahead by the time they neared the top.

As Scrapper John caught up, he heard Sweetwater Eddie whistle, long and low. The mountain man was at the top of the hill, standing next to his horse.

"I ain't never seen nothin' like this before in my life, boy," Eddie called out, his voice filled with awe. "You'd best git up here an' take a look real fast!"

CHAPTER TWO

Scrapper John pulled up next to Sweetwater Eddie and stared down onto the plains below. The grass, growing quickly because of the hot spring weather, lay like an emerald carpet all the way to the next range of foothills. Reaching almost from one end of the plain to the other was a wagon train.

Dozens of prairie schooners, each with a top of bleached, white fabric pulled tightly over a frame of bowed wooden supports, followed one another at a distance of thirty or forty feet. The steel-rimmed wheels cut the tender grass, leaving deep ruts in the dark earth beneath. Men rode on horseback on all sides of the wagons. A small herd of longhorned cattle moved sluggishly off to one side of the wagon train, prodded into keeping pace with the wagons by eight or ten boys on horseback and another dozen children on foot. Dogs were everywhere, barking and yipping, practically racing under the hooves of the cattle and the heavy horses that pulled the prairie schooners.

Woodsmoke curled lazily out of a sheet metal chimney mounted at the rear of a wagon that was longer and wider than the others in the line. The sounds of creaking axles, bawling longhorns, and orders shouted from the men on horses reached across the plain to Scrapper John and Sweetwater Eddie. Musket growled deep in his throat and took a step forward.

"Easy, Musket, don't git all riled up," Scrapper John said, not moving his eyes from the spectacle below. "How big do you make that train, Eddie?" he asked.

"I'll tell you this, it's a darn sight bigger'n I'd ever care to try to ramrod. Looks to me like there's a hundred or more wagons. An' look— they've got a herd of beef with them, an' a remuda of horses, too."

"Remuda?" Scrapper John asked.

"Yeah. Spanish or Texan or some such word, I reckon. It means the bunch of horses the riders ain't usin', kinda like spares an' restin' mounts, so's a man always has a fresh horse."

Suddenly the lead wagon pulled to a stop and one by one, those behind it followed suit. The men on horseback raced toward the wagon, and the boys handling the cattle cut the herd back toward the line of prairie schooners, pushing them hard, shouting and yelling at the cows to speed up. A half-dozen men broke away from the lead wagon. The sun sparkled on the barrels of the rifles they carried. They spaced themselves out in a long line and rode quickly toward the rise where Scrapper John and Eddie watched.

"What's goin' on?" Scrapper John asked. "Seems like they're all in a lather 'bout somethin'."

"It's us they're in a lather about, John," Eddie muttered. "They seen us and they wants to know if we're friend or foe. We'll start down to meet them. Keep your hands in sight an' keep that wolf of yours close an' quiet, hear me?"

Sweetwater Eddie nudged Zinger with his heels. The chestnut stallion began picking his way carefully down the steep slope. Scrapper John snapped his fingers at Musket. When the dog looked at him, Scrapper John motioned with his right hand to Black Lightning's side. Musket moved into place.

Scrapper John nudged Black Lightning down the slope right behind Sweetwater Eddie's horse. The line of men from the wagon train drew closer, riding at an easy lope. They sat on their horses comfortably and well, John noticed. And they cradled their rifles across their chests, supported by their right hands. It looked casual but the weapons were ready to fire in a split second. These men were not tenderfoot sodbusters. They knew their way around horses and firearms.

When Sweetwater Eddie reached the bottom of the rise where the flat grassy plain began, he jogged Zinger forward a few yards and stopped. He took a corncob pipe from the pocket of his deerskin shirt, struck a sulphur match on the sole of his moccasin, and puffed clouds of fragrant tobacco smoke into the warm air. He seemed totally unconcerned about the approaching riders.

Scrapper John drew up next to the mountain man. "Kind of a hard-looking welcoming party," he said.

Eddie puffed on the pipe, his cheeks puffing as he drew air. "I'd rather travel with a bunch of wagons watched over by gents like these fellas ridin' up to us than with some fancy-pants gunslinger hired in a cow town," he said. Then he nodded toward the approaching riders. "I'd judge these will git their folks where they want to go."

Four of the men reined in. The two riders in the center of the line slowed their horses but kept riding. They stopped twenty feet from Sweetwater Eddie and Scrapper John. One of them was tall and thin, with a hard, unsmiling face. The other, a short, dark-haired man, smiled broadly.

The tall rider spoke first. "My name's Wes Stone. I'm the ramrod of the train back yonder." He peered past Scrapper John and Sweetwater Eddie up the slope behind them. "When are the rest of your men comin' on down?" he asked.

Sweetwater Eddie grinned. "Ain't no others to come down. I'm right glad you asked, though. I'd 'a asked the same question, the same way. My name's Eddie—Sweetwater Eddie. This sprout here's Scrapper John. We're headin' to the Spring Rendezvous of all the mountain folks."

The dark-haired rider smiled. "Pleased to meet you boys. I'm Billy Ketchum. I work for the Union Wagon Transport Company—the folks who put together this here wagon train." His face glowed with pride. He added, "She's the biggest one ever—one hundred and seventeen freighters, almost five hundred souls, an' as many horses an' cattle as most ranches got."

Wes Stone studied Eddie for a long moment, still not smiling. "I don't suppose you'd know how to cook a beaver's gizzard, would you?"

The mountain man laughed loudly, slapping his knee with the hand that held his corncob pipe. "Sure I do—if I'm fixin' to poison myself and die. Eatin' beaver gizzard will put a man in the ground faster'n a Colt .45 will. An' make less noise doin' it!"

Stone smiled for the first time. He eased his horse forward, shifted his rifle to his left hand, and extended his right to shake with Eddie. "No reason for nobody but a mountain goat to know that," he said. "Pleased to meetcha, Eddie." He shook with Scrapper John, as well. "Howdy, John," he said. Nodding toward Musket he added, "Beautiful wolf-cross you got there."

Scrapper John grinned with pride. "Musket's

his name. He's smarter than a whip an' twice as fast."

Billy Ketchum shifted his rifle to his left hand just as Wes Stone had. "You'll eat with us? Won't be much 'cept beef stew an' fresh bread with butter, and coffee strong enough to eat through your gut in a hour."

"Be right proud to," Scrapper John answered. "Neither one of us has tasted cow in some time, an' we sure don't see much butter, neither."

Wes waved his arm in a circle over his head. The four riders in the rear turned their mounts and sprinted back to the wagon train.

"You expectin' trouble, Wes?" Scrapper John asked.

"I'm always 'specting trouble when I'm runnin' one of these trains, son. Thing is, I heard Sun Dog an' a big party of warriors are in the area. I've got some good men here, but the biggest part of the train is shopkeepers and sodbusters who don't know which end of a rifle to point. They're fine people, but they sure ain't Indian fighters. That Sun Dog, he's plain crazy from what I hear. It'd make me real happy to git him in my sights an' be done with him." Stone's voice was hard and cold when he spoke of the Indian chief.

"There you go again, Wes," Billy Ketchum said sharply. "You don't know nothin' about Sun Dog except that he's ridin' with a party of other Indians. You jist up an' assume he's a renegade. Could be that . . ."

"A good Indian is a dead one, far's I'm concerned," Wes snapped.

Scrapper John was about to protest when he caught Sweetwater Eddie glaring at him. He held his tongue.

"There's good an' bad Indians, jist like whites," Eddie said slowly.

Stone grunted and spit off to the side of his horse. He dug his heels into his horse, urging it ahead of the others.

"He's a good man," Billy apologized for his friend, when Wes Stone was out of earshot. "But Sun Dog has him—and all of us, I guess—a little nervous."

There was a great deal of activity around the wagon train when the riders reached it. People were lining up outside the cook's wagon, and young children chased each other, shrieking and laughing. The scent of savory stew drifted through the air, reminding Scrapper John how hungry he was. Several teenaged boys about his age nodded to him and he smiled back. Some dogs rushed toward Musket. The wolfdog growled suspiciously, and bared his long white teeth, bringing them to a swift stop.

A cluster of men and women formed around Wes, Scrapper John, and Eddie. Wes made introductions quickly. "These fellows are mountain men. They're going to eat with us. No reason to fear them."

A little girl in a gingham dress shyly handed a plate and a chipped mug to Scrapper John. "My sister said you're right dashin' lookin'. She

17

said she hoped you and your daddy would eat near our . . ."

A young girl, also in a gingham dress but almost Scrapper John's age, suddenly grabbed the tyke's arm. She had long blond hair, and her face turned crimson as the little girl spoke.

"But you *said* . . ." the tyke continued as her older sister dragged her away, clapping her hand over the child's mouth. A man and a woman stepped forward, both laughing.

"Those two are our daughters, Christine, the baby, and Elizabeth," said the man. "I'm Dave Hildebrand and this is my wife Serena. We'd be proud if you'd care to eat with us."

Scrapper John accepted the invitation quickly, before Sweetwater Eddie had a chance to say a word. Eddie and Dave grinned at each other.

"Load up your plates," Serena said. "That's our wagon right over there—the fourth one after the cook's. I've got some cobbler for dessert, too."

Danny Hildebrand, who was Elizabeth and Christine's older brother, introduced himself to Scrapper John and Eddie. A tall, strongly built, blond youth, he was a few years older than Scrapper John. His handshake was firm and strong, and his eyes seemed to be on the verge of laughter. He grinned at the mountain men and nodded toward his sisters. "Elizabeth there is about half mountain lion an' half timber wolf," he laughed. "You'll see what I mean when you git to know her."

Elizabeth glared at her brother. "Don't listen to Danny," she said. "He's just mad because I could lick him in a wrestling match 'till he was seventeen years old." Her face broke into a smile. "Maybe I still can if he gives me enough reason," she added.

Wes Stone and Billy Ketchum joined the group as they began to eat. Scrapper John finished his first plateful of stew. He lined up with Danny for seconds.

"How does your cook feed all these folks?" Scrapper John asked.

"We do everything in shifts," Danny answered. "And there ain't jist one cook—there's three. They cook about all day an' night. They feed the guards an' night riders at first light, then the rest of us, an' then they start cookin' lunch. Mr. King of that big King Ranch in Texas where they raise those fancy horses sent one of his cooks when he heard about our train."

Scrapper John, who was very knowledgeable about horses, was impressed at the mention of the King Ranch. "Sure is fine stew," he said. "Beats Sweetwater Eddie's cookin' right into the ground. And mine too."

The two boys joined the adults who were eating together beside the Hildebrands' wagon.

"Where are you folks headed with this wagon train?" Eddie asked. "Seems like we're goin' in pretty much the same direction, if you was gonna pass the rise on the east."

"That's what we're going to do," Wes Stone

said. He took a carefully folded map from the pouch he carried on his cartridge belt and spread it on the ground. "The folks in this wagon train own all this," he said, pointing on the map. "Bought it from the government. It's a valley with lots of streams an' a small river. Soil's so good cattle git too fat to walk almost, an' wheat springs up outta it faster'n a cricket in a fire."

He indicated a range of mountains shown on the map. " 'Course, we got to go around these, an' it'll take us five, maybe six days. You boys can ride right on over them. Then we got to cross this river. Our valley is a two-day ride from there."

Sweetwater Eddie set his coffee mug down and looked carefully at the map. "Anybody here actually seen this valley?" he asked.

"I seen it," Billy Ketchum smiled. " 'Bout a year ago, before we bought it. Prettiest place on God's own earth. I been tellin' Wes an' everybody else that it's a paradise, an' that they couldn't find a better place to live an' farm nowhere. Why . . ."

Eddie interrupted, poking his finger at the map. "Is there some kind of wierd-looking rock 'bout as big as a small mountain in the valley? Around here, close to this river?"

"Why yes, there was, now that you mention it," Billy nodded. "Strangest thing you ever saw. It's all rock, and it's shaped jist like a human skull, all gray an' weathered. An' right where the eyes would be if it was a skull, well, there are trails of water all the way down to the ground. It sure looked like that huge ol' skull had been cryin' about somethin' real sad. An' even though it was durin' a dry spell when I seen it, the water was still flowin' from those eyes." Billy Ketchum laughed, but his voice sounded a little shaky. "Kinda spooky, know what I mean?"

Sweetwater Eddie stood suddenly, his coffee unfinished and forgotten. His face was tense, his eyes dark and troubled.

"You men have some real heavy changes of plans to make," he said solemnly. "That place Billy jist described is called Skull Mountain by the Plains Indians. It's the most sacred piece of land anywhere to them. They believe that skull up there is cryin' for all the troubles the tribes have had since the white men came."

He looked directly into Wes Stone's eyes. "The Indians figure trespassin' on that land is a killin' offense, an' there's lots of white men's bones out there to prove they mean business. You can't even take no wagon train through there, much less settle an' farm on it. That's Indian land—sacred Indian land."

Wes Stone looked up, his eyes as hard as Sweetwater Eddie's. "Maybe it was Indian land once," he said. "But it ain't no more. The U.S. of A. owns it now, an' the people who put this train together bought it legal. These folks are goin' to Skull Mountain an' no bunch of Indian nonsense is gonna stop me from getting 'em there!"

"It ain't nonsense to the Indians," Eddie said grimly.

"I told you what we're doin' an' where we're goin'," Stone snapped. "That's the way it's gonna be—Indians or no Indians!"

Scrapper John watched Sweetwater Eddie hold Stone's stare for a long moment. Then the burly mountain man spun on his heels and stomped off into the gathering dusk. Scrapper John swallowed hard in the uncomfortable silence that Sweetwater Eddie left behind.

CHAPTER THREE

Scrapper John and Musket found Sweetwater Eddie squatting next to Zinger, the horse's right front hoof turned upward between the man's knees. The mountain man poked at a small pebble that had lodged between the soft part of the underside of the hoof—called the frog and the harder surface. He grunted to acknowledge Scrapper John's presence without looking up.

"If that land really is sacred like you said, the wagon train don't have a chance," Scrapper John said quietly.

Eddie nodded. "Yeah, you're right. Thing is, I can't figure out what that hardnose Stone meant about buyin' the land. I can guarantee this: the Indians wouldn't sell Skull Mountain to nobody—not even the federal government. But there's been lots of trouble between whites an' Indians since '76 when Colonel Custer and his men got their butts handed to them at the Little Big Horn. Maybe the government jist somehow took it over."

"Then the Indians still believe the land is theirs, right?"

"You bet they do, boy," Eddie answered glumly. "But scarin' the pants off 'a all them people in the train ain't gonna accomplish nothin'—at least not right now."

Scrapper John looked back at the encampment of prairie freighters sprawled across the prairie. "What're we gonna do?" he asked.

"I figure we'll light out for the Rendezvous first thing tomorra, jist like we planned to. Somebody there will be able to tell us jist what's goin' on with Sun Dog. Maybe there's some kind of treaty or somethin'. But I doubt it. I've heard of Sun Dog an' his braves. Him an' a shaman named Tangled Face put together an army of braves from all the Plains tribes. They declared a truce among themselves, an' they're lookin' for a place to settle. They got all their wives an' kids following twenty or so miles behind the braves. Sun Dog's afraid the pony soldiers will shoot 'em up like that lunatic Chivington done at the Sand Creek Massacre in 1864."

Scrapper John scratched absently behind Musket's ears. "We plumb got to do something, Eddie," he said. "I got this strange feeling in my gut that there's gonna be trouble. Big trouble."

Eddie looked up from his work on Zinger's

hoof. "We'll see what we'll see at the Rendez-vous." His face broke into a smile finally, and he winked at Scrapper John. "That feelin' of yours—it couldn't be that you jist ate 'bout fifteen pounds of that stew, could it, son?"

Zinger and Black Lightning had worked up a frothy sweat climbing the rocky mountain ridge. Scrapper John and Eddie had been riding steadily for a day and a half, and had almost reached the valley where the Rendezvous was being held. The first night out from the wagon train, Eddie burned a catch of fine, fat trout almost to cinders, and Scrapper John thought fondly of the stew he'd eaten at the Hildebrands' wagon. Elizabeth, too, drifted in and out of his thoughts. He liked the fact that she enjoyed life on the wagon train trail and wasn't afraid to tussle with her brother Danny.

The heavy thunder of a Sharps Buffalo rifle being fired was the first sign that they were nearing the Rendezvous site.

"Boys are doin' a little target shootin', I reckon," Eddie grinned. He rested his hand on the polished stock of his own rifle, which was tied behind his saddle. "Me an' ol' Susy might jist win ourselves some trinkets an' pelts in one of them contests." He glanced sideways at Scrapper John. "You still keepin' your oath about not never usin' no firearms, boy?"

"Sure am," Scrapper John answered. "My pa swore he'd never use a gun again when he come back after the War Between the States, an' he kept his promise. I took my oath in his memory, an' I'll keep it all my life."

Filtering through the pine trees came the sharp reports of Remington .30 repeating rifles, mixed with loud blasts from the heavier, far more powerful Sharps. Above the treetops, pale smoke from cooking fires drifted into the sky. Shouts and roars of laughter reached the two riders.

"Sounds like the boys are whoopin' it up real good," Sweetwater Eddie observed.

The 1887 Spring Rendezvous was in a low, lush valley, far from any sign of civilization. Above the gentle sweep of land, the mighty peaks of the Rocky Mountains touched the sky. The valley was thick with mountain pine, where generations of grizzly bears had lived without seeing—or even scenting—a human being. It was mid-day when Sweetwater Eddie and Scrapper John came upon the encampment of mountain men and their families. They broke from the forest into a clearing where a jagged line of men dressed in deerskins were firing rifles at a target. One of them stood head and shoulders over the others. Sweetwater Eddie banged his heels into Zinger's sides. The horse shot into a gallop as if he'd been fired from a cannon. Eddie whooped like a maddened Indian, racing toward the big man.

The rifleman spun at the sound of the rapidly approaching horse, a gigantic smile lighting up his bearded face. Eddie cut Zinger to one side and dove from the saddle. He hit the other mountain man, slamming them both to the wet ground with a bone-jolting thud. The other men laughed and went on with their shooting. Cursing joyfully, the tall rifleman wrestled Eddie face downward and stuffed his face into the muddy ground.

"Sweetwater Eddie, you never could wrestle much better'n a fat kitten. I oughta trim your hide right off an' take it home with me!"

Eddie squirmed under the larger man, barely able to contain his laughter. "Not on the best day you ever had, Jim Walker! I've fought better men than you when I was still in diapers!"

Scrapper John rode up on Black Lightning as the two men scrambled to their feet and embraced like a pair of fighting bears. Then they stood apart at arms' length, beaming at each other. Eddie looked up at John. "This here's my old pal Jim Walker. And Jim, this sprout is Stone Pete Lewis's boy, Scrapper John."

"Right sorry to hear 'bout your pa an' that one-eyed grizzly," Jim Walker said, turning to Scrapper John. "Stone Pete was a good man. Say, are you half the fighter your pa was?"

Scrapper John grinned. "Well, I reckon I can hold up my end of a . . ." That was as far as he got. Jim threw himself at the boy, hauling him out of his saddle and carrying him into the mud. The two wrestled over and over until Scrapper John, roaring with laughter, was pinned back down, with Jim's knees on his shoulders.

"You ain't too bad a scrapper for a pup," Jim

bellowed. Musket's harsh, menacing growl stopped the mountain man. He looked up at the wolf-dog's yellow eyes ten feet away. Musket looked as if he were ready to pounce.

"Your dog don't seem to care for me settin' on you, Scrapper John." His voice showed no fear at all, only interest. "He's trained right good. Bring him over."

Jim let the boy up and they both stood, dripping mud. Scrapper John motioned briefly with his hand and Musket raced to his side. The dog kept his eyes locked on the mountain man, still growling deep in his throat.

"He's a friend, Musket," Scrapper John said quietly. The growling stopped but the dog's suspicious eyes didn't leave Jim Walker for a second.

"You done a good job with him," Jim said, eyeing Musket carefully. "Your pa was good with animals an' I can see you got that from him." He punched Sweetwater Eddie on the shoulder. "That's my fire over yonder," he said. "You can hobble your horses out beyond it. Help yourselves to the grub in the pot. I'll be over directly, soon's I teach this bunch of no-accounts how to shoot."

Scrapper John and Sweetwater Eddie led their horses in the direction Jim Walker had pointed. They found the campsite, and the stew in Jim's pot was as good as what they'd eaten with the wagon train people. Sweetwater Eddie swallowed his last mouthful, belched loudly, and stood.

"I'm goin' to wander some an' see who lived through the winter. These here are good people. Make as many friends as you can, 'cause folks like us got to stick together. Seems like we're kinda dyin' out as a breed, an' we don't want that to happen." He turned and lumbered off.

With Musket at his side, Scrapper John rode slowly around the huge encampment. At each campfire he passed, a mountain man or woman offered him something to eat. When he came upon a rowdy bunch of men with bows firing arrows at a faraway tree, he stopped to watch. The target was a scrap of red cloth wedged under the bark of the tree. It was about the size of a man's palm, and thirty yards away. A breeze carried some of the shots to the left of the mark. Still, Scrapper John was impressed. The men were solid archers. One of them finally noticed him.

"You do any shootin', young fella? You seem awful interested."

"I've done some," Scrapper John admitted, climbing down off Black Lightning. "That target don't look much bigger'n a gnat's eye from here. It's a long shot."

"Sure is." The man's smile grew wider. "What we're doin' here is shootin' for pennies. Each of us gits three arrows, an' we put three coppers in the pot. First man to plant three arrows in the bull's-eye gits the pennies. So far no one's got more'n two in. You fancy givin' it a try?"

"I don't have no pennies," Scrapper John said. He reached into his pocket and took out a rectangular piece of hard, rough stone. "I got me a sharpening bit, though. Will it count for my three pennies?"

The men exchanged looks with each other. A good sharpening stone was worth a lot more than a few pennies. " 'Course it can, son," a second man said. "Here—give my bow a try." He handed over his bow and three arrows from his quiver.

The bow was longer than Scrapper John's own, but didn't seem much more powerful. He notched an arrow and drew the bow to a full curve. A slight breeze touched his cheek. He moved the bow slightly to allow for the movement of the air. Then he released the arrow. The men drew in their breaths as it whipped through the air and stuck dead center in the red target cloth.

Scrapper John smiled slightly, and notched a second arrow. It struck home half an inch from his first, bringing a murmur of excited comments from the men. "No way you can top that, young fella," one of the shooters called out.

"Maybe not, but I can sure try," Scrapper John told them.

He touched the side of his face with a wet fingertip. The breeze made the spot on his cheek feel slightly cooler than the rest of his face. Then he notched the third arrow. He held the bow at full curve for a long moment, waiting for the right moment. When the cool sensation on his cheek stopped, he knew the breeze had died down for a moment. He released the arrow.

It slammed into the tree between his first two shots, so close that the razor edges of its hunting point sheared the side feathers from the arrows on either side. For a moment, there was a surprised silence. Then the men cheered and slapped Scrapper John on the back, shoving the handful of pennies into his pockets. A few minutes later, as he rode through the camp, the coppers jingled pleasantly in his pockets.

Scrapper John came upon a group of boys his own age, mounted on horses. He joined them and introduced himself. One of the boys had fire-red hair and a big smile, and rode a pinto.

"Call me Red," he said. "I seen you ride in. That spotted horse of yours is one of them Appaloosas, ain't he?"

"Yep. I've had him 'bout a year now. Me an' a Blackfoot friend of mine went to a place the Indians call the Valley of the Spotted Horses an' each got us a horse."

"Can that Appy cover any ground?" Red asked.

"He's as fast as greased lightning," Scrapper John grinned. "And he eats pintos for breakfast."

Red laughed and slapped his knee. "I guess we're jist goin' to have to see about that, ain't we, John? We'll race way out to that rise there, beyond the trees, go clean around it, an' then back. It's maybe six miles. If your Appy can't go that far, I'll snug a rope to him an' drag him back for you."

Black Lightning somehow picked up on the excitement of the crowd of boys, dancing sideways in anticipation of the race to come. He snorted and flung his head from side to side. Red's pinto was no stranger to races either. He fought the reins, his muscles tense, his eyes wide with excitement. Some mountain men wandered over to watch. One of them agreed to be the starter.

Scrapper John eyed the rise in the distance. He figured the run would be closer to ten miles each way, not the five or six Red mentioned. Scrapper John snapped his fingers at Musket.

"Stay here, boy. I'll be right back."

Black Lightning felt like a tightly coiled spring under Scrapper John. He glanced at Red and his pinto. The pinto—Stepper, Red had named him—was a fine horse, with a broad chest, well muscled rump, and straight, clean legs. It would be a close race, and a fast one.

The starter pulled a coonskin cap from his head and held it high in his right hand. "I'll count back from three, an' you'll be off at one," he shouted. "You boys run 'em hard but don't bust your horse to win no race." He paused. "Three!" he roared.

Both riders leaned forward, their reins tight against the bits. The horses' legs quivered, ready to launch forward.

"Two!" the mountain man roared.

The two boys held their breaths.

The starter swept his coonskin hat down, shouting at the top of his lungs, "One! Run 'em, lads!"

CHAPTER FOUR

Black Lightning and Stepper lunged forward neck and neck, neither horse willing to give a fraction of an inch to the other. They galloped with their bodies extended and their heads low, their forelegs reaching far ahead in a long, smooth rhythm that allowed for no wasted motion.

Scrapper John and Red rode bent at the waist, their heads close to the extended necks of their mounts. The cheers of the boys and the men watching the race were soon left far behind. Now, all the boys heard was the dull thunk of unshod hooves striking the earth. Both of the riders knew that they'd soon have to check the horses' breakneck pace, or the animals would run until their lungs and legs could no longer support them.

Scrapper John eased back on his reins. Lightning snorted and shook his head angrily from side to side, not wanting to slow down. The Appaloosa pushed at the bit with his tongue, trying to ease the pressure his rider was putting on his mouth. Long strands of sticky saliva flew from his open jaw.

Red was having difficulty slowing Stepper as well. The pinto fought the reins and the bit, whinnying in anger as the boy tried to check the horse's gallop. Neither horse would give in to the other and slow.

Knowing that if their mounts couldn't see each other, they'd be easier to handle, the eyes of the two boys met for a moment. By unspoken but mutual consent, they reined apart, opening the space between the two horses. They'd already covered three miles at a flat-out run. Now, as the riders took charge again, the horses began to work.

Now that he could no longer see his opponent, Black Lightning responded to Scrapper John's cues. The boy slowed the Appaloosa to a ground-eating lope, a gait Lightning could maintain for long periods of time. The hoof beats behind him told Scrapper John that Red had demanded the same pace from his pinto.

The ground was soft in many places because of spring runoff but higher places had been baked hard by the hot spring sun. Scrapper John and Lightning were closing in on the rise. It wasn't high, but it blocked any view of what lay beyond. More and more, the ground was dotted with pebbles and bits of rock. To a shod horse, it wouldn't have made any difference, but neither Lightning nor Stepper was shod.

Scrapper John gazed ahead, worried about the rocks littered across the ground. A horse could easily break a leg on that kind of terrain. He heard the rhythm of the pinto's hoofbeats pick up. Black Lightning snorted, hearing the same thing.

"Red!" Scrapper John hollered over his shoulder, "If the ground gits worse we'll haul 'em in an' call it a tie!"

"OK, John!" Red called out.

John smiled. He liked Red more and more. Not only did the boy love horses and racing as much as he did, but Red also knew that it wasn't worth harming a horse to win a race.

The rock-strewn ground gave way to grass when the riders were about a mile from the rise. Red pushed Stepper to regain the few yards he'd lost to Scrapper John. Lightning was breathing hard but evenly, with no signs of raspiness. Scrapper John gave the Appaloosa another half inch of rein, letting him increase his pace the slightest bit.

The rise was dead ahead. The hill stood against the sky like a gigantic fort. Scrapper John set himself and his horse up for a hard turn to his left, shifting more of his weight to his left stirrup to cue Black Lightning to the direction of the turn. Stepper was coming on fast. The pinto sucked in huge lungfuls of air.

Scrapper John tapped the bit once, lightly, and then put more of his weight in his left stirrup, pressing the rein against the right side of Lightning's neck. The horse responded beautifully. He fired into the turn and came out of it in a run that hadn't lost any speed. Suddenly, with no warning, Scrapper John hauled back on the reins, pulling the startled Appaloosa to a long, sliding stop. The boy vaulted out of the saddle, gaping at the scene that stretched out behind the rise.

Red skidded Stepper to a halt just behind Scrapper John.

"I . . . I ain't never seen nothin' like this before in my whole life," Scrapper John said, his voice trembling in awe.

"I ain't neither," Red seconded, his voice the same as Scrapper John's.

The valley beyond the rise was covered with grass, still yellow from a long winter under snow. A small herd of mule deer stood where they'd been grazing, staring at the horses for a long moment, and then abruptly taking flight. Above the valley, a solitary bald eagle drifted effortlessly on invisible currents of air, searching for prey below.

In the center of the valley a massive stone outcropping looked as if it had been sculpted into a human skull by giant hands. There were dark caves in the rock where the eyes would be, with water filtering from the entrances and flowing down the face of the rock like tears.

"It's about the spookiest thing I've ever saw, I'll tell you that," Red commented.

Scrapper John nodded. "Sure is. I know what

it is—it's a place the Indians call Skull Mountain."

The eye sockets in the giant rock skull gazed down at the two boys and their horses, dark and foreboding. Even Lightning and Stepper appeared to be under its strange, mysterious spell. Instead of standing quietly, dragging in breaths of air, they skittered about nervously, as if they wanted to get away from the presence that haunted the fertile valley.

"I didn't know we were this close to Skull Mountain," Scrapper John said. "This is sacred ground to the Indians, and the Rendezvous is probably being held on ground that's sacred too. If Sun Dog and his warriors hear about this, there's gonna be trouble."

Red tore his eyes away from the brooding skull that loomed above them. "Nobody said nothin' 'bout sacred land to me. You know as well as I do that mountain folks git along with the Indians. The Rendezvous wouldn't have been held here if we'd knowed about this here valley."

He looked about, his worry evident in his eyes. "What do you think we oughta do, John? Don't seem like we can move the Rendezvous now—it's already started, with all the cookfires burned down good, an' everybody settled in an' everything."

"That ain't for you an' me to decide. But we got to get back an' tell the adults 'bout this."

"How'd you happen to know all this stuff?" Red asked.

"Sweetwater Eddie an' me ran into a giant wagon train on our way here. It was headed this way but had to go around some mountains we rode right on over. They had maps an' deeds an' such showin' they owned the land by Skull Mountain. Eddie knew about the skull and wasn't sure if the government bought the land an' then sold it to the wagon train folks."

"What . . . what do you think Sun Dog would do if he found out about the Rendezvous bein' so close to the valley?" Red asked.

Scrapper John swung into his saddle. "I don't know, but I can promise you this: he ain't gonna be real happy 'bout it. You better climb onto Stepper, Red, 'cause now we got a *reason* to run a race."

Red mounted and tugged his pinto's head around toward the end of the rise. "We ain't got no starter this time," he said. "But that don't mean nothin'. Our horses is matched real good. You ready?"

"We're as ready as we'll ever be. One more thing, though. If either of us has to slow down or stop, the other's got to keep goin'. We got to tell everyone about Skull Mountain as soon as we can."

Red nodded. "Let's go!" he shouted, banging his heels against Stepper's sides.

With ten fast miles behind them, the horses were much easier to handle on the way back to the site of the Rendezvous. About half way back, Scrapper John noticed that Stepper's breathing had become less even and seemed

39

louder. Then the pinto began to drop behind. Scrapper John turned in his saddle and waved to Red.

"I'm goin' on," he shouted.

Red returned the wave and drew in his reins, dropping the pinto to a walk to let him recover. Scrapper John and Black Lightning dug across the open prairie toward the Rendezvous site.

Cheers reached Scrapper John's ears as he raced toward the men and boys waiting back where the race had started. Then, Jim Walker and the others saw the tight, anxious look on his face. "You boys be ready to ride out if Red is hurt somehow," Walker told the others. "Maybe somebody ought to fetch . . ."

Scrapper John slid Black Lightning to a stop and swung down from his saddle.

"Jim," he panted, "Just beyond that rise is a big valley with a huge rock skull in it. It's sacred land to the Indians. Me an' Sweetwater Eddie met up with a wagon train . . ."

"Whoa!" the mountain man said. "Slow down an' take it easy an' tell me what happened. Where's Red? Is he hurt?"

As Scrapper John started to explain everything, mountain men began drifting over. Sweetwater Eddie burst from the crowd and rushed up to Scrapper John. He listened as Scrapper John finished telling his story.

Jim Walker put his hand on Scrapper John's shoulder. "You did right in riding hard to git back here an' tell us what you seen," he said. He looked at Sweetwater Eddie. "I never been in these parts before. I heard of Skull Mountain, but didn't know where it was at. The boy says there's a wagon train headed to Skull Mountain. Is that right? Folks is plannin' on settlin' on sacred ground?"

"It's the truth, Jim," Eddie answered. "I been checkin' around with some of the fellas to see if anybody knows of a treaty that might cover the land. Nobody knows about one. Luke Swingle, the fella who picked out this here site for the Rendezvous, he figured Skull Mountain was another fifty miles or so from here. Looks to me like we're all tresspassin' by havin' our get-together here."

Walker nodded. "Looks that way. We gotta git the boys together an' decide what to do. But that ain't the big problem. I'm thinkin' 'bout all them folks in that wagon train headed this way. Who's the bonehead in charge of that bunch? Don't they know no better'n to go bargin' onto sacred ground? They're gonna git their hair handed to 'em, is what's gonna happen."

"A fella named Wes Stone is the ramrod, an' a guy named Billy Ketchum is there from the wagon train company. They both seem like good men. Stone don't seem to have no use for Indians, though." Eddie hesitated for a moment and then went on. "Billy had maps an' a deed that looked real to me. He said his company bought the whole valley from the government, an' he had the papers to prove it."

Walker's grin was hard. "You an' me both know what good them papers'll be if Sun Dog catches wind of all this. Some tinhorn with a fancy suit an' a printin' press musta gone into business sellin' land. Ain't no way in the world the Indians would give up that mountain."

Suddenly, three quick rifle shots broke the conversation. All conversation stopped. A moment of silence followed and then two more shots. It was the signal for trouble. Everyone turned in the direction of the gunfire. A long line of mounted Indian warriors stretched across the horizon, rifles cradled in their arms. Except for the occasional whinny from a horse, there was dead silence.

"Well," Sweetwater Eddie grunted, "Ain't no more worry 'bout the Indians findin' out we're here."

CHAPTER FIVE

Two warriors, both wearing the feathered headdresses of chiefs, rode forward ahead of the line holding their horses to a slow walk.

"That there's Sun Dog an' his shaman Tangled Face," one of the mountain men said grimly. "Looks to me like we got us a right fine passel of problems."

The two Indians stopped their horses about twenty yards from the mountain men. Their rifles remained cradled in their arms, but were menacing just the same. Sun Dog, the taller of the two, had rich, bronze skin and sharp, chiseled features. His eyes were dark and secretive, and his hair hung in two long braids. War paint streaked his face, chest, and tightly muscled arms.

Tangled Face lived up to the name he'd been given when he was born. His eyes bulged from their sockets, liquid black and deeply intelligent. His mouth ran sharply up the right side of his face, leaving his front teeth exposed on the left. One ear was set high on one side of his head, the other seemed too low. Like Sun Dog, his bare skin was striped with war paint.

"That one Indian's sure a ugly pup, ain't he?" one of the mountain men whispered.

"He's Sun Dog's chief advisor, an' he's smart as a whip," Sweetwater Eddie answered.

Scrapper John tried to watch the strange-looking Indian without staring, but he found it difficult.

Sun Dog made a sweeping motion with his right hand, then pointed to his chest with the index finger of the same hand. In sign language, he was telling the white men that he wanted to talk with their leader.

"Jim, you go on out an' jaw with them," a mountain man suggested to Jim Walker. Others took up the idea.

"Go on, Jim," several called out.

Walker looked up at the two mounted Indians. He put his hand on Sweetwater Eddie's shoulder. "You're comin' with me, Eddie," he said. "If I go alone, we lose face 'cause there are two of them an' only one of me."

Eddie stepped up next to Walker. "I ain't much at talkin', Jim, but if you want me to go with you, I will."

Together, the two men strode toward the two men on horseback and came to a stop a few feet away. Jim started to speak in sign language to

44

Sun Dog. The Indian chief made a quick, irritated gesture with his hand.

"We speak English," he said. His voice was cold, and there was an edge of anger in it. His eyes met first Walker's and then Sweetwater Eddie's. "You and your people are on sacred land that has been consecrated by our ancestors, and by the ancestors of our ancestors. Is this a new way to further insult my people? Haven't you already done enough to us by killing our buffalo and stringing fences across our land?"

"I'll tell you this, Sun Dog," Jim said. "I've never strung an inch of barbed wire, nor has my friend here. Nor have any of the mountain people in our camp. And we don't murder buffalo for sport. We're here through a foolish mistake. We didn't realize we was so close to the sacred valley where the skull cries. You've come to us with battle in your eyes, and you accuse us of doin' things we ain't done. It don't seem fair to me. Is it the way of the Indians to blame all white men because some white men have treated you folks unfair?"

A cold smile played at the corner of Sun Dog's mouth. "Tell that to my people, who die from sleeping on the disease-infested blankets the white men gave us."

"None of us here had nothin' to do with that!" Sweetwater Eddie exclaimed. "We're here by mistake, like Jim said. We'll make it right with you if we can, but we'll fight you if

45

we have to. That's up to you. But I'll tell you this, an' you can take it right to the bank—you ain't been in a fight 'til you faced a bunch of mountain men!"

Tangled Face burst into laughter, snorting through a nose which had only one open nostril. "This man is feisty," he said to Sun Dog. "We outnumber them two to one, and this man flies in our faces with proud words! Maybe what we've heard about the mountain men is true."

Sun Dog didn't look at Tangled Face. "You forget that these people are insulting the spirits of our ancestors," he said coldly. "And a boy from their camp has stolen a horse from us."

Sweetwater Eddie's patience was near its end. "Just a blamed minute here, Sun Dog," he growled. "Mountain men an' their families don't steal horses or nothin' else. We . . ."

"Where else would a white boy get an Appaloosa that runs like the wind unless he has taken it from Indians?" Sun Dog interrupted.

"We don't steal nothin'!" Eddie exclaimed. "Tell me what horse you talkin' about an' I'll—hold on! You mean the kid who just rode in on the flashy stud horse?"

Sun Dog nodded. "The horse you whites call Appaloosa. The Nez Perce first bred such a horse, and they raise only the finest now. Our scouts saw this boy . . ."

It was Sweetwater Eddie's turn to interrupt.

"Jist hold on for a second," he told Sun Dog. He waved to Scrapper John, who was standing with the rest of the mountain men watching the strange meeting.

When Scrapper John saw Eddie's signal, he trotted forward.

"Tell Sun Dog here where you got Black Lightning," Eddie told him.

Scrapper John swallowed nervously and looked up at the two Indians astride their horses. "Me an' my blood brother Seeks The Far Sky—he's a Blackfoot—went to the Valley of the Spotted Horses. We caught us two Appaloosas an' trained 'em right there in that valley. Then we rode right on out through a pass what was jist crawlin' with rattlers. We waited 'til there was a good rain storm, an' a flash flood took away most of the snakes for us. Even so, it was a right scary ride."

Sun Dog and Tangled Face listened attentively, their eyes never leaving Scrapper John's face. When the boy finished, there was an uneasy silence. The two Indians looked at each other. Finally, Sun Dog turned to the mountain men and spoke.

"The boy speaks the truth, for only someone who has been to that Valley can describe it. I was wrong about the horse being stolen, and for that I am sorry. But nothing else has changed. You and your people are still on sacred Indian land."

Sweetwater Eddie began to answer but Jim Walker grabbed his shoulder to quiet him.

In a calm, reasonable tone of voice, Walker said, "We already told you we're here by mistake. If we have to, we'll move our rendezvous, but I hope that ain't necessary. We'll be all gone within a few days. We can give you some supplies fer your families, like blankets an' such. We could call it rent if you like— somethin' we give you in return for usin' the land we're holdin' our rendezvous on. We got some fever medicine too, an' you're welcome to that. It's easier for us to git it than it is for you, an' some of your younguns might need it come next winter."

Sun Dog began to answer when Tangled Face motioned him to silence. The two Indians talked in hushed tones, their heads close together. Sun Dog waved his hands angrily, but Tangled Face kept whispering. Minutes passed—then more. It was clear that there was a major difference of opinion between the two Indian leaders. Their faces were grim when they turned back to the mountain men and Scrapper John.

Tangled Face raised his right hand. "It is a fair offer," he said quickly. "We need the blankets and medicine."

"It is charity!" Sun Dog spat, looking at the mountain men with hate-filled eyes.

"No it ain't!" Jim Walker said quickly. "Like I said, it's a trade for letting us use your land for our get-together. Ain't no charity involved nowhere."

Tangled Face spoke sharply to Sun Dog in

their native tongue. Sun Dog's face burned with anger. When they finished speaking, Sun Dog looked up.

"We accept," he growled. "Put the goods together and have everything brought to this spot. And you can thank your Great Spirit that your blood is not staining the ground this very day!"

"And you can thank yours that you didn't have to wrassle with a bunch of mountain men today!" Sweetwater Eddie exclaimed.

Jim Walker and Scrapper John both grabbed at him.

"Hush, you knucklehead!" Jim hissed. "You'll blow the whole deal!"

Bolts of angry lightning seemed to shoot from Sun Dog's eyes. "One day we will fight, mountain man," he snarled, leaning forward on his horse to stare at Sweetwater Eddie. "And I warn you. You have been allowed to escape our wrath. But the next whites who set foot on this sacred land must pay with their lives. And then we will take the goods we have allowed you to give us!"

With those words, Sun Dog spun his horse around and took off in an angry gallop back toward the line of warriors.

Tangled Face watched as Sun Dog raced off. Then he spoke to the mountain men. "Sun Dog is a great warrior and a great leader. Remember this day when you speak to others who may trespass on Indian land. You have tasted mercy, but in the hearts of many of my people, hatred is stronger than a great leader's orders."

Tangled Face's eyes swept across the gathering of mountain men and came to rest on Scrapper John. "Your horse runs well," he said. Then he spun his mount and galloped after Sun Dog.

Scrapper John stood for a moment, his mind racing. He was positive he'd felt friendship in Tangled Face's final stare, not hatred.

As the mountain men walked back to the main campsite, Scrapper John and Sweetwater Eddie told Walker about the wagon train.

"Sounds like bad business," Walker said. "Sun Dog's pride was hurt by havin' to trade with us instead of fight. He ain't gonna take too kindly to a hundred or so prairie schooners and a slew of people settlin' in Skull Mountain, that's for sure. We got to git word to that train, Eddie."

"Me an' John'll find the wagon train, no trouble, Jim," Sweetwater Eddie offered.

Scrapper John nodded, then added in a low voice. "But convincin' Wes Stone to turn back or head somewheres else ain't gonna be easy."

At the main campsite, mountain men and their families closed around them to hear what had taken place. Scrapper John snapped his fingers at Musket and the dog bounded to his side, barking happily.

"What's goin' on with you, boy?" Scrapper

John laughed. "You're actin' like a foolish pup. I've left you longer than this little spell before."

Musket kept jumping about, yipping and whining, and poking his nose into the boy's hand. Scrapper John walked toward the camp he and Eddie had set up in a grove of trees, not far from the main site. One of the boys had led Black Lightning back to the camp, and unsaddled him. The reins were looped loosely around a young tree, and the saddle rested against the trunk.

He sat down next to his saddle and leaned back against the tree. Not far away the mountain people crowded around Jim Walker and Eddie, questioning them and debating the encounter with Sun Dog and Tangled Face. The wives of the mountain men had gathered their children together in case of an Indian attack, and the youngsters were still with their mothers. The rest of the Rendezvous site now seemed deserted.

Scrapper John plucked a tender blade of grass and began chewing on it, wondering when he and Eddie would leave to warn the wagon train. Memories of the Hildebrands—especially Elizabeth—ran through his mind. Then he shuddered, remembering the cold hatred on Sun Dog's face when he galloped off. He tried to shake the memory but couldn't. Then he reminded himself that the danger from the Indians was over for the moment.

He sighed and began to stand, when suddenly the air hissed. Scrapper John froze halfway up from the ground. An arrow quivered in the trunk of the tree, barely three inches from where he'd been sitting!

CHAPTER SIX

Musket frolicked about, whining as if he wanted to play. Then Scrapper John saw the feathers on the arrow—two black and one red. Suddenly Musket's behavior made sense. The arrow could only belong to one person—Scrapper John's blood brother Seeks The Far Sky.

"Sky!" the mountain boy called out excitedly. He choked off the word before it was scarcely out of his mouth, and quickly turned to look at the crowd of mountain people a short distance away. No one had heard. Then, although it was midafternoon, he heard a night bird singing in the forest. He hustled toward the sound with Musket at his side.

Not far into the forest, Scrapper John stepped into a clearing. His eyes lit up when he saw a slender Indian boy standing in the shade of a gnarled oak tree. Seeks The Far Sky matched Scrapper John's smile with one of his own. The two boys embraced and then stood back from one another at arm's length, both talking at once. They stopped, laughed, and then did it again.

"I saw you speak with Sun Dog and Tangled Face. I snuck back here to the woods, but Musket caught my scent right off." Sky grabbed Musket and tussled with the dog, scratching behind his ears. "I have missed you too, Musket," he said.

The Indian boy straightened and faced Scrapper John. The blood brothers were the same height and build, but Seeks The Far Sky's skin had a deep, coppery hue, and his long, black hair fell straight down his back. A single feather dangled from his beaded headband.

"Much has happened to me since we left the town of Burnt Rock, Scrapper John," Seeks The Far Sky said. "When you went back to your cabin, I returned to the Blackfeet people, just as I told you I would. I found many changes and all of them were bad. There was hunger and sickness. And many of the braves had flat eyes—eyes that no longer saw a reason to stay alive. There was much of the white man's whiskey, too."

The Indian boy looked away from Scrapper John for a moment, fighting the emotion building in himself. When he spoke again, there was a slight tremor in his voice. Musket whined, as if he recognized Sky's sadness.

"The braves said that the Blackfeet people— and all Indians—were doomed by the white man. They said that rifles and fences and trains built on iron roads that go farther in a day than a man on a good horse can ride in four days, these things mark the end of the Indian nations. Only two men offered an answer to what the Blackfeet and the other Indians faced."

"Two men?" Scrapper John asked, confused. "Do you mean somebody like the President or . . . ?"

Sky snorted bitterly and his eyes grew hard. "Not white men, not white chiefs who wear fancy clothes in the town called Washington. I mean real leaders—true Indian warriors!"

"Who . . . ?"

"Sun Dog," Sky said, his voice hard and low. "And the one called Tangled Face."

Scrapper John drew a quick breath. "Tarnation!" he exclaimed. "You mean you're ridin' with them crazies?"

"They are not crazy! They fight for what belongs to all Indians. Sun Dog and Tangled Face have brought warriors from all tribes together to reclaim what is rightfully ours! Sun Dog says his warriors will find a home for all the Indian people—and I believe him. That's why I ride with him, my friend."

"What is it that Sun Dog plans to do? He seemed 'bout as friendly as a rattlesnake with a toothache when I last seen him."

"Sun Dog carries many troubles on his shoulders. He says if blood must be shed, it will be white men's blood along with that of the Indi-

ans. The red man will take back what is his—
like Skull Mountain. There are other places,
too."

Sky turned, listening to sounds that filtered
into the forest from the Rendezvous campsite.
People were drifting back to their camp fires
and tents. "I must get out of here before I'm
discovered. I hope you understand why I ride
with Sun Dog, Scrapper John. Do you?"

"I guess so," the boy admitted. "But it seems
to me that there's better ways to git things
done than ridin' with a war party." Scrapper
John's eyes clouded with confusion. "Maybe it's
'cause I'm half Indian that I kinda agree with
you, Sky. It ain't a' easy thing to stand by an'
watch Indians bein' run off land and all that.
But the Indians have killed a awful lot of
whites who didn't want to do them no harm."

The sound of voices nearby caught the attention of both boys.

"I must go," Sky said hurriedly. "You think
Sun Dog is crazy—but he isn't. But he is angry.
I give you this warning because we are blood
brothers, Scrapper John, and nothing will
change that. I have heard from Sun Dog that
a giant wagon train is headed toward Skull
Mountain. That wagon train and all those who
are a part of it are doomed as soon as the train
crosses the river that runs just outside the sacred lands. Their blood will flow upon the soil
of our ancestors. Sun Dog has promised this. If
. . . if there is any way you can turn that wagon
train away . . ."

Sky stopped, drew a breath, and clutched Scrapper John's shoulder. For a moment, the two boys stared deeply into each other's eyes. Then Seeks The Far Sky spun around and ran toward the forest without another word. Scrapper John stared at the spot where his friend had disappeared into the woods. Despite the warm sunlight that filtered down through the leaves, he felt a chill sweep up and down his back. Sky had made one thing certain—Sun Dog and his warriors wouldn't hesitate to attack if settlers went onto sacred Indian land for a second time.

Sweetwater Eddie was scuffing out the coals of the camp fire when Scrapper John and Musket got back to the camp. Eddie's mouth was stuffed with jerky, but it didn't stop him from talking, and it didn't disguise the urgency in his voice.

"You'd best git ready to travel, John. Eat some jerky and drink some of this here coffee. I know you don't much like it, but it'll help you keep awake tonight. We got to head out as soon's we can, and we ain't gonna stop ridin' 'til we find that wagon train. It's up to us to warn 'em—no two ways about that. I wish you wasn't runnin' that horse of yours today 'cause he'll need all the heart he's got for tonight. Is Black Lightning gonna be able to keep goin'? If he ain't, I can borrow you a mount."

"He'll keep goin'," Scrapper John answered without hesitation. "He ain't anywhere near bein' used up." He stepped over to where

Zinger and Black Lightning stood side by side, as if they'd been friends all their lives.

"Least we won't have to worry 'bout these two bitin' holes in each other's hides," he said. "Seems like they've cleared up any nonsense left between 'em."

"Good," Eddie grunted. "This ain't gonna be no pleasure ride, boy. We're gonna be climbin' at night an' coverin' ground jist as fast as we can. We got to git that wagon train turned 'fore it's anywhere near Skull Mountain. That Sun Dog ain't a man to waste words or make promises he ain't about to keep, an' it's a right good bet that them warriors ridin' with him are jist as thirsty for white blood as he is."

"He isn't thirsty for blood," Scrapper John exclaimed. "It's just that the Indians . . ." He stopped speaking when he saw Eddie staring at him curiously.

"What's that you're sayin', John?"

"Nothin', Eddie. We ain't got time to jaw right now. I'll check the horse's hooves an' then saddle them up. You goin' to ask anyone else to ride along with us?"

The mountain man shook his head. "Nah. More riders would just slow us down. And it ain't like we need help findin' a wagon train. It ain't but the biggest thing outside a mountain on the face of the prairie, an' it's got a herd of cattle an' horses with it, an' more people than most towns. I don't reckon it'll up an' sneak past us without us seeing it."

Scrapper John picked up each of Black Lightning's hooves and inspected them. Then he went to the Appaloosa's head and looked into the horse's nostrils. The delicate tissue inside was pink and healthy looking. If the race had been hard on Black Lightning it would have been a dull gray color, showing that the horse had lost too much oxygen from running too hard.

Scrapper John saddled the two horses, setting the girths tighter than he usually did, since they'd be climbing and heading down steep rock faces. If a saddle slipped during that kind of travel, the result could be disastrous to both animal and rider.

As they mounted, some of Sweetwater Eddie's friends wandered over from the main campsite. Word had gotten around the Rendezvous quickly about where they were going.

"You boys keep your hair on your head where it belongs," one mountain man cautioned them. "That Sun Dog feller ain't goin' to think twice about droppin' you if you was to run across him."

"I met Wes Stone one time when I was buyin' supplies in a little burg called Linden Creek," said another. "He's a good man, but he's got a head as hard as a rock when it comes to Indians. He ain't got no use for them at all. From what I hear, he lost a wife an' a couple kids in a Indian killin' raid right after the War Between the States."

Sweetwater Eddie's face tightened. He turned to Scrapper John, his dark eyes troubled. "That ain't gonna make Wes no easier to convince that he should turn back," he said.

"But that was years ago. It . . ."

"John, a man don't never forget somethin' like that, no matter when it happened. You won't ever forgit that one-eyed grizzly that did your pa in, will ya?"

Scrapper John thought for a moment, and then nodded. "I guess not. Let's ride, OK?"

Eddie set the pace as the two rode out of the Rendezvous camp. They held to a fast lope, covering ground well but not tiring the horses as a gallop would have. The mountain range loomed ahead of them, with jagged, snow-covered peaks poking into the blue sky.

Eddie changed their direction slightly and then rode dead at a V-shaped cleft in the wall of rock halfway along the horizon. The lowest part of the V would be where they'd make their climb over the range, and descend on the other side.

Every half hour, Eddie called for a stop to rest Black Lightning and Zinger, and after a while he slowed the horses from a fast lope to a slower one.

"Gonna need all the strength they got before long," he told Scrapper John.

The sun was at the horizon when the two riders began to climb. The wind had sharpened, and their faces quickly turned red from the cold, stinging gusts. The ground changed from prairie dirt to rock. Musket, jogging next to Black Lightning, picked his way carefully over the sharp stones but didn't slow his pace. As they drew rein at the first steep slope of shale and soil, Sweetwater Eddie stopped and dismounted. He tugged a bag of jerky from his saddlebag and stuffed a handful of the dried meat into his mouth. He tossed the cloth bag to Scrapper John. The boy fed several thick knots of meat to his dog. All three chewed in silence for several minutes, their eyes drawn to the slope.

"Don't look like nothin' we can't handle," Scrapper John said optimistically.

"That's jist what Colonel Custer said back in '76 at the Little Big Horn," Eddie grunted. He looked at the darkening sky and frowned. Scrapper John followed the man's gaze

"What's the matter, Eddie? You thinkin' we're gonna run into some bad weather?"

The mountain man didn't take his eyes off the sky. "No, I don't think so. Not right away, anyhow. The thing is, I got a bad feelin' 'bout this early spring. I ain't real sure winter's over yet, John. We could be in for a real mountain-buster of a storm 'fore it's done with. Sure is gittin' a piece colder, ain't it?"

He checked Zinger's cinch and mounted up. "Gimme a bit of room ahead of you, an' stay off to one side. Ol' Zinger's gonna be throwin' bits of rock behind him an' there's no sense in you gettin' knocked silly by a flyin' hunk of stone." He grinned. "It'd slow us way down if I had to stop an' douse you with water to wake

61

you up. Keep that wolf of yours close to your side, too."

Scrapper John snapped his fingers and pointed next to Black Lightning. Musket, who'd been sniffing at a prairie dog hole, trotted over and took his position. Eddie started up the slope at a trot, using his heels against Zinger's sides to keep him moving. The big stallion's hooves scrambled for traction on the shale-like surface, putting a cloud of fine dust into the air. Lightning dug in the same way, slipping as his hooves dislodged rocks.

"Git your feet outta your stirrups, John!" Sweetwater Eddie yelled back over his shoulder. "If your horse starts to go down you git off—he's better off without you in a fall." He added, "You're better off without him on top of you, too."

Scrapper John nodded. "Yeah," he called out to the mountain man. "I'd sure hate to hurt this good Appaloosa by havin' him fall on somethin' as hard as me."

Eddie grunted. "You might make a mountain man yet, boy."

Both horses were working hard. The slope was steep and getting steeper, and the footing was sloppy. Scrapper John was uncomfortable with his feet out of his stirrups but he knew Eddie was right. With the light fading, the shadows grew longer and deeper. Off to their side, a small stream was filled with spring runoff. Mist sprayed into the cold air as the icy water slashed over rocks and boulders.

The wind lashed at the riders and their horses. As the man and boy climbed higher, an icy sleet began to pelt down.

"It ain't quite snow," Scrapper John called out to Eddie. "But it sure ain't sunshine, neither!"

Eddie turned in his saddle and looked back at Scrapper John. "Sometimes you git jist as feisty as my ol' pard Stone Pete, boy. An' I'll tell you this—there ain't many full growed men I'd want ridin' with me right now 'stead of you."

Scrapper John smiled but said nothing. The compliment made the cold and the whistling wind easier to take, though. As they rode on, his mind slipped back to his talk with Seeks The Far Sky, and he shuddered. The wagon train—Elizabeth, Christine, Danny, and Mr. and Mrs. Hildebrand, and all the families heading for Skull Mountain—made Scrapper John want to push Black Lightning for more speed. He was glad Eddie was ahead of him on this trip.

Sweetwater Eddie reached the summit ten yards before Scrapper John and dismounted. He stood next to Zinger and gazed out over the other side of the mountain. The boy could see the mountain man's grin.

"Come on up here an' have a look," Eddie called. "There ain't too much of a question 'bout where the wagon train is at."

Scrapper John climbed down from Black Lightning and led him the last few feet to where Sweetwater Eddie stood. The prairie stretched endlessly to the far horizon. Far below them and to the east, a giant circle of flickering, orange camp fires glowed in the dark. Musket whined slightly. Barking, too faint for humans to hear, reached his sensitive ears.

"We found them all right," Scrapper John nodded. "Now we just got to talk them into turnin' and goin' back the way they came."

CHAPTER SEVEN

By the time the two riders had picked their way down the far side of the range, the sun was threatening to rise and early morning sounds could be heard from the wagon train. Horses in the remuda whinnied for a ration of grain, and the night riders were drifting in for coffee from the cook.

Sweetwater Eddie stood in his stirrups and sniffed appreciatively. "I can smell good coffee from farther away than a hawk can see a fat hen sleepin' in the sun—an' that's right good coffee I smell."

He eased Zinger into a lope, not pushing the horse, but picking up the pace. Scrapper John followed. Black Lightning was suddenly alert as the scent of strange horses reached him.

"You'd think Stone would have a better guard out than . . ." Eddie began.

A rifle slug whistled over their heads, cutting off the mountain man's sentence. He reined Zinger to a stop.

"We're friends!" Eddie bellowed. "Tell Wes Stone that Sweetwater Eddie and Scrapper John Lewis are out here!"

"No need to tell me nothin'," a voice on their left called out. "I been watchin' you two ride in for a good long time."

Scrapper John and Eddie turned their horses in that direction. Not far away, Wes Stone sat on his horse, rolling a cigarette. The two riders rode over.

"Good to see you boys. Come on in—Cookie will have grub an' coffee ready by now." Stone gazed up at the sky, which was beginning to color with dawn. "Or he should have, anyway. Half the day is shot already."

"Don't you ever sleep?" Eddie asked, chuckling. "Last time I heard, a ramrod didn't have to draw no night ridin'."

There was no laughter in Stone's voice. "I sleep when I need to. We been seein' signs of Indians—lots of them, all mounted—an' I don't like it."

Stone swung his horse toward the wagon train, leading Eddie and Scrapper John into the camp. Billy Ketchum stood at the huge coffee urn, a mug steaming in his hand. His smile was wide and welcoming.

"Eddie! John! Real good to see you. What brings you fellas back this way? You decide to buy into the valley an' be farmers?"

"Not hardly," Scrapper John laughed. "We ain't the farmin' kind, Billy. Thanks anyway."

The arrival of the two riders brought a crowd of curious settlers from their wagons. Those who'd met Scrapper John and Eddie a few days earlier called out greetings. Eddie got down from Zinger and walked to the coffee pot. He poured himself a cup of coffee and drank half of it in a single long swallow, although the liquid was scalding hot. Then, as people gathered around, he turned to Scrapper John.

"Maybe you oughta do the talkin', boy," he said. "Sometimes I git kinda het up an' don't say what I mean."

Scrapper John looked at the assembled group and then fixed his eyes on Wes Stone's.

"There's real big trouble ahead for this here wagon train," the mountain boy said loudly. "Sun Dog's ridin' with a bunch of braves who're out to take back Indian land from the white men. These braves mean business. Sun Dog and his counsellor Tangled Face are jist bristlin' for a fight, an' that Skull Mountain place is sacred Indian land. They'll attack anybody who ain't a Indian who sets foot on that land!"

Wes Stone hadn't gotten down from his horse. He tossed the nub of his cigarette into a puddle of spilled dishwater.

"We ain't turnin' back an' we ain't turnin' off," he said harshly. "No pack of crazy Indians lookin' for trouble is goin' to scare me off. I'm gettin' paid to take this wagon train to that mountain an' I'm goin' to do it. An' I'll tell you

67

this. I'll deal with that Sun Dog—one on one or any way he wants it."

Stone spun his horse. "I got work to do!" he snarled over his shoulder as he galloped away from the cook's wagon.

Eddie, his face livid with anger, stepped toward Zinger. "I'll chase that hothead down an' explain the facts of life to him, darn his hide! This ain't some personal battle he's fightin' with one Indian—he's got the lives of hundreds of people in his hands!"

Billy Ketchum put himself between the horse and Eddie. "You ain't gonna do nothin' but cause more trouble if you ride after him now, Eddie," Ketchum said. "Give Wes a little time to chew things over in his mind an' talk to him later on in the day."

A red-haired lady with a baby in her arms stared at Scrapper John, fear written across her face. "Is what you said true? About an Indian attack?"

A tall, lean, young man stepped up behind the lady. "Missy—what's the matter? Did I hear you say something about Indians?"

"There sure could be, ma'am," Scrapper John answered. "I don't want to start no panic, but . . ."

"Then maybe you ought to keep your yap shut, youngster, 'cause startin' a panic is jist what you're gonna do!" snapped a heavy man with a holstered Colt at his side. "We don't need no rumors botherin' folks on this wagon train."

"Wait—let the boy talk," another settler demanded. "We all got a right to hear about anything that could mean trouble to the wagon train."

"An' I say we don't waste time listenin' to no scared little kid!" the heavy man growled. "Wes Stone is the ramrod here, an' we'll jist do what he says! As for you, boy . . ." He reached out to grab Scrapper John's shoulder.

Sweetwater Eddie's voice boomed. "It's a real good bet that boy can trim you down to size his ownself if you touch him, mister, but if he can't, then I will!"

Billy Ketchum stepped into the middle of the fracas, his arms raised high. "Eddie! Vince! You boys got nothin' to fight about. Nobody said Wes couldn't handle trouble—but all of us know how he feels about Indians."

"Wes Stone's hate could get all of us killed!" a woman shrieked. Her voice was so loud and shrill that for a moment there was total silence. Even Sweetwater Eddie and the heavy man, whose name was Vince, stopped glaring at one another and looked at the woman. Billy rushed to her and led her to one side, talking quietly to calm her. Scrapper John stepped over to Sweetwater Eddie.

"We got to talk to Wes," he said. "An' you twistin' this fella's tail ain't gonna do nothin' for nobody."

The mountain man, his eye narrowed and the line of his jaw rigid under his beard, thought for a moment. "Yeah," he finally agreed. "You're right, Scrapper John. But I ain't about to stand by when one of my friends is bein' pushed around."

The people who'd gathered began talking again, but quietly, from time to time glancing cautiously at Scrapper John and Sweetwater Eddie.

"John! And Eddie!" a female voice called out. "I knew you'd be back! I was just telling Dave that very thing yesterday morning."

Serena Hildebrand, almost dragging little Christine behind her, rushed up to the cook wagon. Her voice sounded as pleasant and cheerful as it ever had. "I hope you'll be spending some time with us. You rushed off too soon after we first met." She turned her happy smile to Scrapper John. "And Elizabeth hasn't talked of much but you since you left, John."

She gasped when she realized what she'd said. "I'd have tied my own mother's braids in knots if she'd said anything like that to my Dave when we first met! You forget I said it, OK?" she told Scrapper John.

The crowd had broken up and people were drifting off to their wagons.

"Already forgot," the mountain boy grinned. He looked around quickly.

Dave Hildebrand, a bit of lather on his chin from his morning shave, strode up and shook hands with Sweetwater Eddie and Scrapper John. "Good to see you men back," he said. "We got us a river crossing coming up first thing tomorrow morning, and it'll be right handy to have you along. Danny's been working getting our wagon secure.

"River?" Sweetwater Eddie asked. "I don't recall no rivers 'round here that take much more'n steppin' over, Dave."

"It's about twenty miles due east, and you're right. It isn't much of a river, except in springtime. Our scouts said it's runnin' like a steam locomotive."

Scrapper John's heart beat crazily in his chest. He hadn't realized the crossing was so close. "It's like you was sayin', Eddie. This kind o' warm weather at this time of year is real strange. Seems like all the snow ain't ready to melt yet, an' there's so much water the ground an' streams an' such jist can't handle it."

Eddie nodded. "That's true. An' I'll say it again—I wouldn't bet that ol' man Winter's given up an' run off for the year. I think we're gonna see him again 'fore it's all over."

"I hope not," Serena Hildebrand laughed. "I've packed our woolens at the bottom of our trunks and I'd hate to have to plow through all our things to find them. But there's no sense in worrying about the weather right now. You two must be starved. Come back with us to our wagon and I'll see that you get a decent breakfast."

That brought a smile of appreciation to the faces of both Scrapper John and Eddie. As they walked over to the Hildebrand wagon, Elizabeth's voice rang out angrily.

"I told you what I'd do if I caught you in here again! Now you're in for it, you thief!"

Alarmed, Scrapper John rushed to the wagon, where he was struck in the chest by a fluttering, squawking rooster that had been flung out the back flap by Elizabeth. "And stay out you miserable old—"

She cut her words short and broke into gales of laughter when she saw the startled look on Scrapper John's face, and the feathers in his hair. "John! Oh, I'm sorry! I didn't mean to hit you with that rascal."

Breakfast included fresh eggs from the four hens the Hildebrands carried with them, pan-fried potatoes, wheatcakes with molasses syrup, and large servings of canned peaches. Even though he was thoroughly enjoying the extra attention Elizabeth Hildebrand was paying to him, Scrapper John felt his eyes closing with fatigue. Sweetwater Eddie caught him stifling a yawn.

"You'd best git some shut-eye," he said. "Looks to me like we're goin' to be with the train for at least a couple of days, an' you ain't gonna be no good to nobody, if you're dozin' in the saddle."

Scrapper John's eyes brightened. "A couple of days?"

Eddie nodded. "Leastways 'til we can talk Wes Stone into turning it around."

"You both can bed down in our wagon," Dave said. "The train will be rollin' out in a half hour or so. I got work to do, but Serena an' the girls will make you comfortable."

Eddie stood up and stretched. "I'll help out gettin' the freighters ready for the crossin'," he said. "I don't need no sleep jist now. I got some talkin' to do with Wes Stone later on, too. But John, you take these folks up on their offer."

Scrapper John began to protest but then realized that he was falling sleep on his feet. He stretched out in the wagon on some blankets Elizabeth laid out for him. Soon, the wagon train started moving, and the gentle rocking of the prairie schooner over the flat terrain lulled him into a deep, dreamless sleep. Musket, stretched out next to his master, slept just as soundly.

When Scrapper John's eyes popped open he was amazed to see that it was long past midday. He rubbed his eyes for a moment and jumped out of the wagon. Musket leaped out right behind him. The mountain boy noticed that his saddle was riding on the tail piece of the wagon. He looked closely at it. The leather had a rich sheen to it. A scuff it had taken the night before had been fastidiously worked away with rubbed-in tallow.

"Your saddle needed a little attention, John," Elizabeth said with a smile, stepping around the side of the wagon. "I spent a couple of minutes polishing away that scrape. I saw what good condition you keep your gear in, and, well, I didn't really have anything else to do but keep watch over Christine. I hope you don't mind."

"Mind?" Scrapper John laughed. "I sure don't mind, Elizabeth. Thanks very much. I was goin' to take care of that scrape myself today. My pa taught me to take good care of my things so I could depend on them." He looked closely at the saddle. "You done a fine job, too. I couldn't have done no better myself, an' I been takin' care of leather things ever since I was a pup."

Elizabeth smiled at the compliment. "So have I, Scrapper John," she said, her eyes laughing. "Don't think that just because I'm a girl I'd faint at the thought of a little work."

Scrapper John began a hurried and apologetic answer when Sweetwater Eddie rode up and motioned the boy out to him. Elizabeth waved and returned to her duties.

One look at Eddie's face told Scrapper John that his friend wasn't happy. "What's the matter?" he asked. "Did you talk with Wes again?"

"No," Eddie answered. "I figured we'd catch him later on an' try to talk sense to him. What's got me worried is that I've been watchin' the hills real close-like. We got a big bunch o' Indians doggin' us!"

CHAPTER EIGHT

When the wagon train rolled to its final stop for the day, the strange rushing sound of slow, distant thunder took the place of creaking wood and squeaking axles. Riding on horseback several hundred feet out from the train, Scrapper John turned in his saddle to look quizzically at Sweetwater Eddie.

"It's hard-runnin' water, John." The mountain man looked out across the prairie. "Not much sense in ridin' out to have a look-see. It's gettin' dark an' we don't know where Sun Dog an' his men are at. That river will be there in the mornin'. You can bet on that."

The evening passed quickly. Dinner that night was prairie stew, as it was called by the wagon train party, and it contained a bit of just about everything they carried that was edible. Several kinds of meat, from chicken to salted pork, had simmered for most of the day, along with potatoes, carrots and onions, and the herbs that grew wild for the picking. There was lots of thick crusted bread, still warm from baking, to sop up the juices with. And Serena had a special treat for her family and Eddie and Scrapper John—servings of preserved apricots.

After they'd eaten, Sweetwater Eddie and Scrapper John walked along the huge circle of wagons, looking for Wes Stone. They found him running a cleaning rod through a Winchester .30 caliber rifle. He looked up as they approached.

"I don't think we got nothin' else to say to each other. Save your breath an' don't start preachin' at me."

"Ain't your sorry hide we're worried about," Sweetwater Eddie said coldly. "You're puttin' a slew of innocent lives in big danger, Wes. Them folks all trust you, an' you're leadin' them right along to a bloodbath!"

Several men walked over, drawn by Eddie's voice. Three of them carried rifles like the one Wes was working on.

"You mountain people ain't the only ones who know how to fight," one man said. "We can look after our own—with these." He held his rifle out in front of him.

Scrapper John's eyes burned with anger. He couldn't keep silent a second longer. "You men are kiddin' yourselves! Sun Dog's a seasoned warrior. He'll wipe out the wagon train on his first charge—an' it'll be your fault, Wes.

Yours—and theirs, too. Them rifles don't mean nothin' against Sun Dog's warriors!"

"You're wrong, boy," Wes Stone answered hotly. "These men ain't been in Indian fights—but I have. I know all about it. They'll listen to me an' follow my orders an' we'll run that skunk off like the stinkin' coward he is!"

Scrapper John and Eddie glared at Stone for a long moment and then turned away.

"A man can't argue with a lunatic," Sweetwater Eddie growled to Scrapper John. "We might jist as well save our breath. Now, we got to think of some way to turn this train, 'cause Wes is too wound up in his hate to see what he's doin'."

They walked back to the Hildebrands' wagon without much more conversation. Dave had a good sized fire going, and the children were popping kernels of corn. Scrapper John and Eddie sat near Dave and Danny.

"We couldn't get nowhere with Wes," Eddie said. "The man is so jammed up with hate, he can't think straight when it comes to Indians."

"We done the best we could," Scrapper John added. "But Eddie's right. We didn't get nowhere."

Dave Hildebrand looked over at his wife for a moment before he spoke. "Serena don't agree with me on this, an' Danny doesn't, neither. But I gotta go along with what Wes says. There ain't no doubt he hates Indians—but he's still the best ramrod a wagon train could have. He's brought the biggest train that ever was put together a lot of miles without no major problems."

Dave hesitated a moment, looking at Scrapper John and Sweetwater Eddie. "Maybe you folks who live in the mountains git a little too nervous about Indians. Could be this Sun Dog is more talk than anything else. I . . ."

Scrapper John was on his feet in half a heartbeat. "He ain't jist talk, Dave! An' thinkin' he is could git lots of people killed!"

"The boy's right, Dave," Sweetwater Eddie said heatedly. "You're thinkin' of Indians like the ones you see sellin' blankets around settlements an' so forth. Sun Dog ain't like that, no more than a tame, city dog is like a timber wolf."

Dave's response was cut off by a sudden gust of wind that whirled sparks from the fire into the air. The wind had a bite of cold to it that couldn't be ignored. Soon everyone around the Hildebrands' fire—and all the other travelers who were sitting around their own fires—prepared to turn in. Fires were quickly scuffed out and folks headed for the relative warmth inside their wagons.

"Look," Dave Hildebrand said just as Scrapper John and Eddie were about to head off. "I don't want to argue with you. You've got your feelings about this whole thing, an' I've got mine. Let's git some sleep an' maybe things will look different in the morning. It's got too darn cold out here all of a sudden, an' we're gonna have a real busy day crossing that river tomorrow."

He grinned, first at his wife and son, and then at Scrapper John and Eddie. "Lots of the people in the train figure that any danger from the Indians will be behind us once we get across that river. It makes sense to me."

"Sense? I never heard nothin' so boneheaded in my life!" Eddie exclaimed, frustration ringing in his voice. "How can you . . ."

Three rapid rifle shots from one of the night-riding guards abruptly killed the conversation. Then there were three more from a different direction.

"Serena! You an' the girls git in the wagon!" Dave shouted. "Danny—fetch my rifle and grab the Colt for yourself!"

Scrapper John and Sweetwater Eddie bolted to their horses. They jerked the hobbles loose and slipped on their bridles, not bothering to saddle up. Side by side they rode hard toward the first set of shots.

"I can't figure this," Scrapper John shouted to Eddie over the thunder of hoofbeats. "I didn't think Indians would attack at night."

"They usually don't," Eddie called out. "Could be that Sun Dog an' his boys jist plain don't care about them old rules!"

Billy Ketchum galloped up next to Scrapper John, his eyes wide and his face white with fear. Several other men pushed their horses into the group. Some of the riders carried pistols and there were a few heavy caliber rifles strapped into saddle rigs.

Riding at the head of the pack, Scrapper John and Sweetwater Eddie cut between a pair of wagons to the prairie outside the circle. Eddie held up his arm to signal a stop. The moon was hidden behind scudding clouds and the riders had to set their reins hard to avoid slamming their horses into one another. In a moment the clouds passed and the riders stared out at the murky darkness.

Four men on horseback sat in a line twenty yards away. One of them held a spear with a white feather at the end, whipping in the wind. Wes Stone, holding his horse to a slow walk, rode out toward the line. Eddie nudged Zinger with his heels, but Scrapper John cut Black Lightning in front of his friend's horse.

"Eddie," he said hurriedly, "You an' Sun Dog almost got at each other's throats the last time you saw each other. Maybe I should go out with Wes."

Eddie chewed on his lower lip, glancing quickly across the distance at the Indians. "Maybe you're right, John," he said after a moment. "Me an' Sun Dog an' his men sure don't take to each other real well, an' one thing we don't need is more trouble. You go ahead an' I'll hang back here an' keep these fellas in order."

Scrapper John used his heels to launch Black Lightning into a gallop. "It's Scrapper John Lewis comin' up behind you, Wes!" he shouted.

Billy Ketchum rode hard after Scrapper John. Hildebrand and a couple other men rode up behind them moments later. When the mountain boy drew rein next to Wes, he gasped in surprise. One of the Indians was Seeks The Far Sky, riding next to Tangled Face. The two other Indian riders were strangers. The boys' eyes met, but there was no need for words. Any sign of recognition would only cause more confusion and trouble in a situation that was already like a keg of gunpowder about to blow.

The cold wind whipped dust and grit into the air around the two groups of horsemen. When the horses snorted their breath gushed from their nostrils like plumes of smoke.

"I will say but few words," Tangled Face began. His voice was rock hard. "My leader, Sun Dog, sent me. He says he will no longer speak to white men. But he also said he would give your wagon train a chance to turn back. The land you are headed for is sacred to all Indians. If you enter it, your blood will run like the tears on the face of the skull that watches over our land."

Wes Stone's eyes were slits as he glared at the Indians. "I'm gonna tell you two things," he growled, his voice heated with challenge. "I ain't scared of you or your leader. That's the first thing. This is the second!"

He leaned from the side of his horse and spat on the ground. For a moment, all was silent. What Stone had done was the worst possible insult to any Indian.

Tangled Face reached to the head of his spear with a hand that trembled in anger and tore the white feather from it. "You have been warned," he said. "We will not warn you again. If a single wheel of one of your wagons touches the soil on the far side of the river, we will attack and kill you."

He let go of the white feather, and the wind whipped it away into the darkness. "I have spoken for Sun Dog. And I have spoken for myself and all the warriors who ride with us!" Tangled Face wheeled his horse about and galloped across the prairie, with Sky and the other two Indians at his heels.

"My pa didn't raise me up to be disrespectful to adults," Scrapper John said, turning slowly to face Wes Stone. "But what you jist done was the stupidest thing I ever seen. You ain't fit to ramrod no wagon train, Wes—you're too fulla hate that comes pourin' outta you!"

"John!" Dave Hildebrand shouted. "You watch your mouth, boy!"

"He's right!" Billy Ketchum hollered at Dave and Wes Stone. "The boy was one hundred percent right! You didn't leave the Indians no out—now they gotta attack us at the river."

"Jist a minute here," Stone said calmly. "I needed to show them red-skinned cowards that we ain't scared of them, an' I done jist that. If they was gonna ride on us, they'd have done it by now. They was looking for some kind of handout—maybe some of our cattle or somethin'. Now they know we won't be pushed around."

Several of the men nodded in agreement. Others looked like they sided with Scrapper John and Billy Ketchum. More riders from the train pulled up as the argument continued.

Vince, the man who'd had the run-in with Sweetwater Eddie, sat on a tall gray horse, chewing on a cigar. He listened for a few moments without saying anything. Then he called out to Stone. "How come we got a deed for this land we're headed for an' them Indians claim it's some kind of a special place to them? Ain't that fancy legal deed we got no good?"

" 'Course it's good," Dave Hildebrand answered before Stone could respond. "It's our land, fair an' square. We bought an' paid for it, an' it's ours!"

"Sure it's a good deed," Stone said. "An' we got better things than pieces of paper to consider." He pulled the collar of his jacket up closer around his neck. "We ain't got the time to do nothin' but go ahead, deed or no deed. We got to git to Skull Mountain and start building and puttin' crops in the ground before long or the whole settlement won't make it through the first winter."

Voices rose in agreement, drowning out the words of others who were more afraid of Sun Dog and his warriors.

"But Wes," Billy Ketchum protested. "We can't try crossing the river tomorrow. Those braves will cut us to pieces. Didn't you see one of them was carrying a Winchester? There are bound to be other rifles. We'll be sittin' ducks!"

Stone's face flushed with anger. "I'm right sick of your whinin', Billy. An' I'm sick of your mountain man friend an' his smart-mouth pup, too! I'm still the ramrod of this outfit, an' my word is still the law." He looked around at the group of men. "You boys best git back to your wagons an' git some sleep. We're gonna be busy tomorrow."

Scrapper John and Billy Ketchum rode back to the train side by side. Sweetwater Eddie rode up to meet them, his face tense. "What happened?" he asked. "I seen the Indians ride off like their tails was on fire."

Scrapper John and Billy filled him in quickly. Eddie shook his head sadly from side to side. "There ain't no doubt now there's gonna be a fight—not after Stone's spittin' like he done. It ain't me I'm worried about, nor even you, Scrapper John. It's all them women an' kids who're part of the train. They don't have no part in this—but that won't make no difference to Sun Dog an' his warriors when they swoop in for the kill!"

CHAPTER NINE

Scrapper John and Eddie spent the night wrapped in blankets near the coals of the Hildebrands' fire. They kept their horses hobbled nearby, inside the circle of wagons. It was still dark the next morning when Eddie nudged Scrapper John's shoulder with his boot. "Goin' to waste the whole day sleepin', boy?"

The first thing Scrapper John noticed when he threw back his blanket was the temperature. It was much colder than it had been the night before. And the wind had picked up too.

"I'd say we're in for a storm," Sweetwater Eddie said, rolling out of his blankets. "A big one, too. I can't tell where it's comin' from 'cause the wind is changin' direction every few seconds, but it's comin', all right."

The mountain man peered up at the sky. "I can't say exactly when, neither, but I figure it'll hit 'fore the day is out. You grab somethin' to eat an' saddle up, John. We got to help git these wagons across the river." Sweetwater Eddie strode off in the direction of the cook wagon.

Scrapper John was rolling his blanket when Wes Stone rode up and dismounted. "Eddie around, John?" he asked. Although his eyes were red rimmed from lack of sleep, his voice contained none of the harshness of the night before.

"He went over to the cook's wagon for coffee," Scrapper John said. "But I don't think he wants to see you, Wes. He thinks what you done last night was jist as bad as I do."

Stone stood next to his horse for a long moment. "Somethin' you an' your friend Eddie got to understand. My job is to git this wagon through to that piece of land with the skull-shaped mountain on it. That's what I'm gonna do. I might 'a been a little hot with you last night. But what really matters is the river crossin'. Can I count on you an' Eddie to help out?"

"You can count on us," Scrapper John answered. "But only because we ain't goin' to leave the wagons. Them folks is gonna need help when Sun Dog attacks, an' me an' Eddie are gonna be here for 'em. An' that's gonna happen, Wes, jist as sure as the sun comes up in the mornin'."

The man and the boy stared into one another's eyes for a long moment. Then Stone swung into his saddle. "I don't much care about your reasons, boy," he said. He spurred his horse and rode down the line of wagons.

Scrapper John trotted over to the cook wagon, looking for Eddie. He figured it was about time they got a look at the river. He found his friend talking with Billy Ketchum and Dave and Danny Hildebrand. Billy suggested they put their differences aside for as long as it took to get the wagons across the river. Everyone agreed that was a sound idea. They all knew the crossing was going to be a rough one, and that they'd need one another's help.

A few minutes later the men rode out to look at the river. What was a shallow lazy stream during most of the year had become a wildly running torrent because of the heavy, spring runoff of melted snow. Although it was still not more than a couple of feet deep in places, the treacherous, driving water concealed deep holes that could swallow a wagon and the animals pulling it. The water was icy cold—in fact, it had been ice and snow not more than a day ago.

Sweetwater Eddie, Dave Hildebrand, and Billy Ketchum located the best site for crossing, a place where the river curved and was fairly shallow, while Danny and Scrapper John secured the Hildebrand wagon.

"Ain't really the depth that's got me worried," Sweetwater Eddie said, looking out into the churning water. He pointed to a huge splintered log swept along by the water. "Look there—that tree's big enough to stave in the side of a wagon or knock a horse an' rider silly." He turned to Billy. "You got to post men with rifles upstream an' tell 'em to cut loose with three quick shots if anything big is headed down here. Least we'll have some warnin' an' be as ready as we can be. Won't help a wagon out in the middle, but we'll know trouble's comin'."

Billy nodded. "Good idea. I'll tell the men three shots for anything comin' downstream, and four for Indians."

The crossing started as soon as the sun was up. Except for coffee, there was no breakfast since the cook wagon had to be closed up and secured for its trip across the rapids. The horses and oxen pulling the wagons balked at the sound and sight of the water, but the drivers forced them ahead, snapping long whips over the backs of the animals, not actually hitting them, but popping the ends of the whips to urge the beasts forward.

Some of the settlers weren't experienced enough at driving their rigs to make it across. Eddie and Billy took the reins on these wagons, urging the frightened animals into the freezing cold water and across to the other side.

Wes Stone seemed to be everywhere at once, giving orders, driving wagons, helping with panicked horses or steers, and, all the while, checking the horizon for signs of Indians. Scrapper John had to admire the ramrod's efficiency. He kept the wagons moving and stopped his people from doing anything that might cost them their wagons or their lives. And Stone had put the wagons on full alert. The train was most vulnerable to attack while the wagons were in the water or split between the two sides of the river.

Scrapper John spent most of his time on Black Lightning keeping the cattle bunched in a tight herd while the wagons crossed. Four other boys rode with him, doing what they could with the mounts they had. The cattle were nervous, spooked by the sound of the water, and Black Lightning was the only horse quick enough to cut off panicked attempts at bolting away. Scrapper John wore a heavy leather coat Dave Hildebrand had given him to keep the cold out. He rode with the thick collar turned up around the sides of his face. Even so, the wind stung like a lash when it struck bare skin. And it was getting stronger. The canvas tops of the covered wagons whipped and strained in the wind, loose pieces snapping crazily, popping like pistol shots.

Scrapper John was cutting a rank, old milk cow back into the herd when he heard four rapid rifle shots followed by shouts of alarm.

"Keep 'em tight!" he shouted to the other boys. He hauled Black Lightning around in a grinding half circle and raced to the river. On the other side, one of the half dozen or so wagons that were the first to cross was a blaze of fire, and thick smoke rose above it. Wes Stone stood next to the flaming wagon, working the lever of his rifle and firing at the backs of three Indians galloping toward the cover of a small hill.

Scrapper John started Black Lightning into the water along with several others on horseback. Stone stopped firing and waved them back.

"Stay there an' do your jobs!" he shouted, his strong voice almost drowned out by the sound of the wind. "They're gone an' no one was hurt!" Behind him, a bucket brigade had started and the flames that engulfed the burning wagon were quickly extinguished.

"He's right," one of the riders grunted. "We got jobs to do so let's do 'em. The Indians is gone now."

"Sure they're gone now," another answered. "But we'd have to be darned fools to think there ain't a whole bunch more of 'em out there jist waitin' to attack. That ramrod of ours is gonna git us all killed!"

Scrapper John hustled Black Lightning back to where he'd left the cattle, leaving the men to argue. He looked up at the sky as he rode and his heart dropped. Thick gray clouds rolled across the horizon. He urged a bit more speed out of his mount. If the bad weather and Indian attacks stampeded the cattle he didn't think he'd be able to locate half of them. He worked Black Lightning around and around the ragged herd of cows, bunching the frightened animals together as tightly as he could.

When the Hildebrands were next in line to

cross, Scrapper John left the cattle in the care of four other riders and jogged Black Lightning over to the wagon. Dave was in the driver's seat, his face grim and reddened by the wind and the cold. Elizabeth, with her arms wrapped tightly around Christine, peeked out from behind her father. Serena was inside making sure all their goods were solidly tied down.

Scrapper John forced a calm smile at Elizabeth. She tried to return it, but her eyes showed just how frightened she was. Scrapper John eased Black Lightning into the water at the side of the wagon so he could help out if help was needed. He heard a loud cracking sound and something whipped past his face, spooking Black Lightning into a panic. Then another object flashed by, and another, accompanied by shrill squawking. It was the Hildebrands' hens. The fourth hen whipped past, blown by the wind and slammed into the roiling water. Scrapper John used all the skills he had to calm the Appaloosa stallion. Lightning's instincts told him he should be hiding from weather like this, not setting out to swim in a turbulent river.

When Scrapper John finally got his horse under control, he saw that the fabric on the side of the Hildebrands' wagon had split the length of a long seam. Some papers and a book whipped out, followed by some clothing. Scrapper John caught a quick flash of Serena inside, slamming the lid of a large trunk. Against the power of the wind and water the big wagon was puny. It rocked on its leather springs as the wind buffeted it back and forth.

Scrapper John rushed into the deeper water beyond the wagon, loosening the rawhide thong that held his lariat in place. He built a loop quickly and swung it over his head, waiting for a lull in the wind to make his throw. When the lull came he threw the loop hard and fast. It smacked sharply against the front corner of the wagon and dropped neatly over a stout support used to carry a water barrel.

He wrapped the rope around his saddle horn and urged Black Lightning away from the wagon, toward the opposite shore. The rope stretched as tight as a guitar string, but held. It was the little extra bit of help the horses pulling the wagon needed. Slowly, the rig began to move again, still rocking from the wind, but forging ahead through the water.

Both Black Lightning and Scrapper John were panting by the time the Hildebrands' wagon was on solid ground. He waved to Dave, freed the rope from his saddle horn, and swung back into the water, leaving his lariat behind. The boys he'd left to tend to the cattle had done their best, but the animals had broken out of their tight cluster and were running aimlessly, panicked and trying to escape the punishing cold of the wind.

As Black Lightning struggled out of the water, a brindle bull, insane with fear, charged at the horse, head down and his horns out. Scrapper John frantically reined to his right.

The wild-eyed bull hurtled past like a locomotive out of control and surged into the swirling waters. In a heartbeat the animal was flung onto his side. For a moment two of his legs showed above the cold, brown water. Then he was gone.

Scrapper John pushed Lightning into a tired lope, gathering cattle and driving them toward the water. On the banks of the river, Sweetwater Eddie, Danny, Billy, and several of the other men herded them in, yelling to keep them moving. It was slow, tough work. The wind howled, and cold rain began to pelt down, stinging bare skin. The temperature continued its plummet, quickly turning the rain to bits of ice.

Three hours after the last wagon was on the other side of the river, the final cow was hazed across. Men, boys, and horses were soaked to the skin with water so cold that it left their hands and feet numb. In the company of others, Scrapper John rode herd around the miserable cluster of cows until they were relieved by fresh riders. He swung Black Lightning to the cook wagon and gratefully accepted a steaming mug of hot chocolate from the cook. He took a long, burning-hot swallow, and looked at Sweetwater Eddie, who was dripping wet. The Mountain Man's beard was stiff and coated with ice. A few snow flakes were swirling in the air and the wind howled mournfully.

"We got 'em across," Scrapper John said.

"An' maybe this weather will keep Sun Dog holed up for a bit."

Eddie looked out at the craggy mountain peaks in the distance. "Sun Dog ain't our biggest problem right now. Look out yonder."

Scrapper John turned and followed Eddie's gaze. A curtain of snow had swept past the mountain peaks and was racing across the prairie toward the wagon train.

CHAPTER TEN

Within minutes it was impossible to see more than a few feet in any direction. Driven by fifty-mile-an-hour winds, the snow battered the wagon train.

Wes Stone ordered the wagons to pull as close together as possible. He rode from wagon to wagon, almost blind, counting on his horse to see what he couldn't. Soon, the wagons were brought into a lopsided circle.

"We'd best git as many fires goin' as we can," Scrapper John shouted over the howling wind to Wes. "This storm ain't gonna quit soon. We can't have folks freezin' to death in their wagons!"

"Yeah," Stone agreed, shouting into the boy's ear. "There's wood an' a half barrel of lamp oil in the cook wagon for them that can't git a fire goin'." He turned to Sweetwater Eddie. "We need some riders to keep the cattle together," he told the mountain man. "Can John handle that? It ain't gonna be easy, but he sure knows what he's doin' on that horse of his."

"Don't worry about Scrapper John," Eddie declared. "Any youngster raised in the mountains ain't afraid of work, an' they know how to take care of themselves an' their animals, too."

"OK," Wes agreed. "You tell him he's the cattle boss from now until this storm's over. When do you figure that'll be?"

Eddie's grin was cold and without humor. "Long about July, from the looks of it. How much food are the folks carryin'?"

The wind seemed to be getting stronger and louder every minute. Stone had to lean close to Eddie to be heard. "There's food for a week or so, but no more. Most of the space in the wagons was given over to seed an' farm tools. We ain't about to starve anytime soon, but I'd planned on bein' at Skull Mountain right 'bout now. We could live off the cattle for a spell, while crops was growin'."

Eddie grunted pessimistically. "You ain't gotta worry about livin' for long at Skull Mountain, Stone. Sun Dog'll see to it that you don't need much food."

"Least we don't have to worry 'bout no Indian attack in this," he shouted over the screaming storm. "But if we have to, we'll fight them Redskins durin' this here blizzard an' put an end to 'em!"

Sweetwater Eddie grabbed the wagon boss

by the shoulders and jammed him up against the side of the wagon. "That bunch of warriors will go through you an' these settlers in a half minute, Stone!" he roared. He glared into the ramrod's eyes for a moment. Their faces were only inches apart. Then he shoved the man roughly away.

"I ain't got time to argue with a madman," Sweetwater Eddie growled. "I heard about your wife an' your kids an' I'm real sorry. But that don't mean me an' Scrapper John gotta stand by an' watch you kill all these folks 'cause you're lookin' for revenge!" He spun around and started to walk away. "I got work to do helpin' these people," Eddie shouted over his shoulder. "Maybe I can keep of few of 'em alive through this here blizzard, even if it's only for Sun Dog to kill 'em later!"

On the other side of the wagon, Scrapper John was helping Dave Hildebrand, Danny, and other men tie down the canvas wagon tops. Eddie pulled him aside and shouted into his ear. "Has Black Lightning got anything left?"

"He's tired," the boy answered, "but he'll work."

Quickly, Eddie told him he was cattle boss. Scrapper John lurched into the wind and scrambled from wagon to wagon until he found Black Lightning tied to the spoke of a wheel. He swung into his saddle. He was pushing his horse harder then he wanted to, but he had no choice. Cattle were essential to the survival of the wagon train, and they had to be taken care of.

Black Lightning, his eyes squinting against the pellets of snow, slipped on patches of ice as he attempted to settle into a lope. Scrapper John rode toward a small rise, figuring that the cattle, even in a state of panic, would instinctively try to put something between themselves and the wind. After a long and howling whiteout that brought Lightning to a complete stop, Scrapper John saw two other riders heading six or seven cattle back toward the wagons. One of them, his face bloody from a wound on his forehead, cut his horse over toward Scrapper John.

"Indians come on us as we was moving the herd," he shouted. "Wasn't too many of them an' we scared 'em off with rifle fire, but they spooked the herd. There's beef all over the prairie out there! Where's the rest of the riders Wes sent out?"

"Ain't no others I know 'bout. He'll git men out here when he can spare 'em," Scrapper John yelled over the wind. "Where'd the herd break up?"

The horseman pointed to the far side of the rise. The boy waved and rode in that direction. When he rounded the rise he had to drag Black Lightning to a sliding stop to avoid ramming into a dozen or more cattle huddled together, their whiskers white with ice, their eyes closed against the wind.

Scrapper John turned them and started driving. It was slow going. The cattle's instincts pulled them back to the shelter of the low rise, but the way the wind was changing, the best place for them was inside the circle of wagons, where they could be kept moving if necessary, so they wouldn't freeze to death. He wished he had his rope when one of the cows made a run back to the rise, but the lariat was probably still hanging from the Hildebrands' wagon. He cut off the ornery animal and chased her back to the herd.

There were only a couple of hours of daylight left. That frightened him. Any cattle and riders away from the wagons at night during the storm wouldn't have a chance. Off to his right, two riders with eight or ten cattle came into view. Scrapper John kept his charges bunched and waited for them to catch up. They combined their cattle and drove them a mile toward the wagons without losing a single cow on the way, but it took them almost two hours.

Once the cattle were inside the circle of wagons, Scrapper John reined Black Lightning around and started back out. A shout from Wes Stone stopped him.

"Nobody goes out no more 'til mornin', John. It's too dangerous." The ramrod moved closer to make sure he could be heard. "I hate to have to give you this order after you done so good with the cattle, but I'm gonna put you on guard duty tonight—all night. Them Indians is goin' nuts, attackin' durin' a storm like this. I need somebody who ain't gonna panic every time the

99

wind howls. Stick close to the wagons an' keep movin'. I'll git somebody to relieve you when I can."

Scrapper John used his heels to start Black Lightning out into the wind again. He was tired and so was his horse, but he didn't question the order.

There were fires blazing close to many of the wagons. The wind was too strong for them to be very big, but the settlers used crates and barrels to shelter the flames, and huddled close by them. The ragged circle of fires glowed eerily in the swirling, wind-driven snow. Scrapper John was making his second circuit of the wagons when a familiar voice called to him. He came to a quick halt.

"Elizabeth!" he shouted over the wind. "What are you doin' out here?"

She was wearing a long, wool coat and thick mittens, and a pair of her brother's pants. Musket was at her side. When the wolf-dog saw Scrapper John, he bounded up against Black Lightning's side, pawing at his master's leg.

"I'm doin' the same thing you are, John!" Elizabeth shouted. "I'm standing a watch. I can give an alarm as well as you can!"

Scrapper John jumped down from Black Lightning and stood next to her. "I'm sure you can give an alarm," he said, patting Musket and trying to calm the dog. "But it ain't your place to be out here! This is man's work. You go on back to your wagon where you belong!"

Elizabeth's eyes blazed. "Don't you tell me

what to do, Scrapper John Lewis," she told him. "I can guard every bit as good as you. An' if you think I can't, you're just as crazy as that owl I just heard hooting in the middle of this here blizzard."

"What?" Scrapper John shouted. "You heard a owl?"

No owl would fly in a storm like this. It meant only one thing—Seeks The Far Sky was out nearby, and looking for him!

Elizabeth, startled by the urgency in Scrapper John's voice, stepped back. "It was just a few minutes ago—over there, behind the wagons," she said, pointing into the swirling snow.

Scrapper John made a fast decision. He moved close to Elizabeth, talking directly into her ear. "That owl you heard was a Blackfoot friend of mine who's riding with Sun Dog. He's my blood brother. If he's callin' to me, there's somethin' important he wants me to know. Can you show me where you heard the owl?"

Elizabeth grabbed Scrapper John's hand in her own. "Of course I can," she shouted over the roar of the wind. "Come on!"

Scrapper John quickly tied Black Lightning to a wagon wheel on the side away from the wind and followed Elizabeth out into the storm. He snapped his fingers at Musket, and the wolf-dog followed closely. In moments, they were well beyond the circle of wagons. The wind whipped against them.

"It came from right around here," Elizabeth shouted. "I heard it maybe five or six times.

The wind got too loud but then I heard it again."

Scrapper John's throat was raw from shouting to make himself heard, but he did his best to hoot. He strained to hear a response, but the howl of the wind was too much to overcome. It was impossibly dark away from the fires. Scrapper John shivered and tried again. This time, his hoot was even weaker. He lowered his hands from his mouth and stood shaking in the cold wind.

"Elizabeth, you got to go back now. If Sky sees you he might not understand an' he'll think I was forced into setting up some kind of trap for him. What you done is great, but you gotta leave now. You understand, don't you?"

"I . . . I guess so, John. But . . ."

"Please, Elizabeth! This could be real important to all of us—to the whole train!"

Elizabeth was silent for a moment. "I know you wouldn't lie to me, John," she finally said. "I'll go back. And I promise I'll keep your secret. Be careful now, you hear?"

She turned back toward the wagons and in a moment Scrapper John could no longer see her. When he and Musket were alone, he raised his hands to his mouth.

"Sky!" he roared at the top of his lungs. "Sky! Over here!"

Musket, standing at the boy's side, suddenly came to attention. Suddenly the snow parted, and Seeks The Far Sky stepped in front of Scrapper John. Musket yipped a greeting and ran forward. The Indian boy was shivering and his face was a pale spot in the darkness.

"I had to come to you, my friend," Sky shouted over the whine of the wind. "Sun Dog has decided to attack the minute the blizzard is over, and all the warriors agree with him. There's no reasoning with him. I'm afraid, Scrapper John. Too many people will die—both Indians and whites. I had to give you this last chance to convince your people to go back as soon as they can. If you're ready to move as soon as the storm slows and you get far enough away, you might be safe. Go and tell those settlers . . ."

A sudden, desperate thought flashed in Scrapper John's mind. "Can you git me to Tangled Face?" he asked.

Sky paused. "Yes. But why? What can you and Tangled Face do? Sun Dog has made up his mind. There's no turning back for him now. He has visited with our ancestors in a dream and they told him that he should attack and kill the whites who trespass on the sacred land."

"Tangled Face ain't no killer. I know that from when I talked to him before. And I got to talk to him again."

"If that's what you must do, I'll take you," Sky said.

The two boys walked into the raging storm, Scrapper John following closely at Sky's heels. He marveled at how the Indian boy could find his way through the swirling snow and wind.

It took less than an hour to reach the Indian camp. As they snuck past tipis, Scrapper John heard children crying. He heard a woman say, "It is no fault of yours, my husband, that we have no food . . ."

The wind picked up again, drowning out the woman's words. As they passed another shelter, he heard some braves arguing angrily. "It is the white man's fault our families are starving!"

A moment later, Sky led him to a tipi where Tangled Face waited. A small bed of coals gave off heat and dim light. The Indian warrior sat cross-legged, meditating. A smile pushed up one side of his twisted face when Sky pushed through the tipi flap, followed by Scrapper John.

"Somehow I knew we would meet again, young friend," he said to Scrapper John. "I hoped it would not be on a field of battle. But tell me, why have you risked your life coming here? Has your friend Seeks The Far Sky not told you that Sun Dog plans to wipe out the wagon train as soon as the storm lifts?"

"Yessir, Sky told me. I thought we would meet again, too. My ma was a Nez Perce, and sometimes I don't know if I'm a Indian or a white. That don't matter right now, though. I came to see if there is anything I can do to stop Sun Dog from attacking."

Tangled Face looked into Scrapper John's eyes for a long moment. Then he sighed. "There is no way to appeal to Sun Dog in favor of the wagon people, I'm afraid. His hatred for the whites burns, just as your leader's hatred for us burns."

"But it ain't all of us who hate Indians . . ."

Tangled Face held up his hand to stop Scrapper John. "I know this. But Sun Dog's lust to see white blood flow is stronger than any argument you can present."

Loud voices sounded outside the tipi. Tangled Face looked toward the noise. "You must go. If you're discovered here, even I won't be able to help you. Go with this warning. If you are to live, you must leave the wagon train. We will attack as soon as the storm clears. I tell you this because you are the blood brother of Seeks The Far Sky. Now, leave this place before you are discovered!"

Scrapper John turned to Sky. "Tangled Face is right. I got to leave. I . . . I know you got to be with your people, Sky. It scares me real bad to think that the next time we see each other might be in a battle. What if we have to fight . . ."

Scrapper John's voice cracked. He swallowed and then started again. "We might not see each other again. If we don't, remember this. I'm right proud to be the blood brother of Seeks The Far Sky."

Sky looked deeply into his friend's eyes. "And I am proud to be the blood brother of Scrapper John Lewis," he said, his voice husky with emotion. "I must stand alongside my people. But I promise you, I will not raise a weapon against you."

The boys came together in a silent embrace. When they stood apart, Sky said, "We must leave now. I will guide you back to the wagons."

The journey back was swift and hard. Fifty yards from the wagon train, Sky turned back without another word.

Scrapper John and Musket burst between two wagons and rushed toward the largest fire, over by the cook wagon. The wind slowed in the shelter from the encircled wagons. Scrapper John saw Sweetwater Eddie about to mount up on Zinger.

"Eddie!" he hollered.

"Where you been, John?" Wes Stone bellowed angrily. "You git your horse an' git mounted—Elizabeth Hildebrand went out for firewood an' she never made it back! If you'd been on guard duty like I ordered you, maybe that dog of yours coulda picked up a scent. Now, it's probably too late!"

CHAPTER ELEVEN

"Have . . . has anyone . . . maybe she . . ."
The storm swallowed Scrapper John's stuttered
words. On his journey from the Indian camp
back to the wagon train, the wind had been
whipping snow into blankets of whiteness that
were impossible to see through. But unless
they found Elizabeth, she'd freeze long before
the storm was over.

Sweetwater Eddie stood next to Scrapper
John and hollered over the howl of the storm.
"I figure the best bet we have is to use Musket to sniff out Elizabeth. There's about six-
dozen dogs along with this here wagon train,
an' there ain't a single one of them worth his
feed when it comes to trackin' like Musket
can."

Dave Hildebrand's hand trembled as he
tugged a scarf more closely around his head,
covering his mouth. "I've been out behind our

wagon an' fanned out from there, but I didn't see nothing but blowing snow."

Scrapper John took a deep breath and spoke, his voice reaching over the endless scream of the wind. "I ain't sure even Musket will be able to pick up a scent in this wind, and with this much snow blowin' around. But he'll sure try." He turned to Elizabeth's father. "I'll need somethin' Elizabeth wore a lot—like a shoe or dress."

Dave Hildebrand nodded and rushed off toward his wagon.

Scrapper John leaned down and scratched Musket's head. Then he knelt and spoke to the wolf-dog quietly. "Looks like it's up to you, boy."

He stood and stepped close to Eddie. Making sure no one else could hear, he spoke into the mountain man's ear. "I should have told you where I was goin'. Seeks The Far Sky . . ."

"Here." Hildebrand ran up with a knitted mitten in his hand. "This is Elizabeth's—she was wearin' it most of the day 'till Serena gave her thicker ones she found in the trunk."

He handed the blue mitten to Scrapper John. Suddenly tears began to run from his eyes and his body shook with great, wrenching sobs. "You've got to find her," he gasped. "Serena's crazy with worry. Every time a gust hits she thinks she hears Liz—but it's never nothin' but the wind. An' little Chrissie is scared to death for her sister. I told them to stay right inside the wagon an' not to move."

"You done the right thing, Dave," Scrapper John said. "We don't need nobody else lost in this storm, an' that's what would happen if your missus went out lookin' for Elizabeth."

He knelt next to Musket, and carefully wiped the frost and ice from the wolf-dog's muzzle. Then he put the mitten close to his nose. "Find her, Musket," Scrapper John said. "Find her fast!"

Musket sniffed at the mitten once, and then a second and third time. Then he trotted away from Scrapper John, moving slowly, his nose testing the air. A gust carrying sharp pellets of snow struck him full in the face but he didn't seem to notice. He walked slowly out beyond the wagons, nose held high. Scrapper John followed a step behind the dog. Sweetwater Eddie and Dave and Danny Hildebrand followed behind Scrapper John.

For an hour, they struggled through the blinding snow, following Musket. The wolf-dog tested the air with every step. Sweetwater Eddie put his hand on Scrapper John's shoulder.

"It's no good, son," he said, his face close to Scrapper John's. "Ain't a dog in the world who could pick up a scent in this weather. I think we ought 'a turn back. That way, you an' Musket had best git some sleep an' be ready to go back out as soon as the storm dies down."

Scrapper John nodded. He called Musket to him and crouched next to the dog. "You done your best, fella," he said. "Eddie's right. We'll be out here again, soon's the storm gives us a break." He stood up and faced the two Hildebrands. "I . . . I'm sorry. He jist can't pick up nothin'. There's too much wind an' too much snow. We got to wait out the weather. There's no other way."

Scrapper John's voice gave way, and his words were replaced by deep sobs. Anyone out in a storm like this would freeze to death in a matter of hours. By then, Musket would find only a cold, stiff body. And he couldn't avoid the terrible knowledge of his last meeting with Elizabeth. If he hadn't asked her to take him to where she'd heard the owl she'd be sleeping in her wagon right now, not buried under several feet of snow in the middle of a desolate prairie.

When they returned to the wagon train, Scrapper John and Sweetwater Eddie wrapped themselves in blankets in a supply wagon. Scrapper John didn't think he'd be able to sleep, but exhaustion took over. Musket pushed close to him. During the remaining hours of night, Scrapper John moaned several times in his sleep, waking both Eddie and the dog. Sweetwater Eddie stared at the boy in the murky darkness but didn't wake him. Once, he reached over and tucked the blanket more closely around the boy.

The next morning, Scrapper John opened his eyes and heard a silence outside that somehow seemed as loud as the screaming wind had been the night before. He leaped to his feet, startling Eddie and Musket.

"The storm's over!" he shouted. "Come on! Let's git out there!"

Sweetwater Eddie stood and looked out the rear of the wagon. "All right," he said. He added slowly, "You know there ain't much of a chance, don't you?"

"There's always a chance, Eddie. Let's go."

Dave and Danny Hildebrand looked like they hadn't slept at all. Wes Stone and Billy Ketchum didn't look much better. They met at the cook's wagon, and after quick cups of scalding hot coffee, the party set out.

Huge drifts of snow glistened in the bright sun, rolling across the prairie like waves on the ocean. Every so often a patch of buffalo grass showed through where the relentless wind had scoured the drifts away. It was still bitter cold, but the wind had died almost completely.

Musket stopped short, sniffing the air noisily. He paced, with his nose high, in a wide circle. His eyes were almost completely closed and his mouth gaped open. He sniffed at the air, and sorted through the scents. Scrapper John and the others stood dead still, watching, holding their breaths.

Musket whined and pawed at a snowdrift. Then he barked and scrambled across the snow as fast as he could run. Scrapper John raced after the dog, kicking his legs high through the deep snow.

Musket stopped at a high drift and circled it, barking frantically. Then, he tunneled into the snow with his forelegs, throwing a white cloud into the air. Scrapper John dropped to his knees and dug with the dog, shoving snow aside, plunging his arms into the mound. Sweetwater Eddie dropped to his knees next to him. Wes Stone, Billy Ketchum and the Hildebrands joined them.

Soon Scrapper John caught a glimpse of stiff buckskin. Eddie reached in front of Scrapper John and tugged hard at the stiff, cold shape.

"Hey!" he grunted. "It's a kid—an Indian kid!"

"Leave him there!" Wes spat. "We ain't out here to dig up Indians."

"There's something under . . . it's Sky!" Scrapper John shouted. "Elizabeth is underneath him!"

They dug faster, throwing snow in all directions. Moments later, Sweetwater Eddie lifted Sky from the white grave. The Indian boy was unconscious, his bronze skin almost white from the cold. Curled underneath him in her heavy coat, Elizabeth lay as if she were sleeping. Dave Hildebrand clutched at his daughter, hugging her close.

"She's breathing!" he shouted. "Thank God— Elizabeth is alive!"

"This here kid is gonna make it, too," Eddie said, carefully laying Sky down. "An' I'll tell you what, Dave. You'd best thank him for savin' your daughter's life, 'cause that's what he done. If he hadn't laid on top of her with his body she'd have frozen to death."

Scrapper John rubbed Sky's face gently, until the boy's eyes opened.

Sky focused on his friend's face. For a moment he looked puzzled. Then he recognized Scrapper John. "The girl?" he asked softly. "Is she . . . ?"

Elizabeth, still in her father's arms, moaned.

"She's all right, Sky," Scrapper John told him. "You saved her life."

"When I left you last night, the girl and I almost ran into each other. She was lost. Soon I was too, and the storm was growing worse. I dug a shelter in the snow and let it cover us. With the heat from both our bodies, I knew we might live through it."

Elizabeth struggled to consciousness. "Papa," she said weakly, her eyelids fluttering. "Is the boy all right? He . . ."

"He's jist fine, Elizabeth!" Scrapper John bellowed. "An' he ain't jist a boy—he's my blood brother Sky, the one I told you about last night!"

Billy Ketchum approached with blankets, and soon the boy and girl were wrapped tightly in them. Slowly the party of settlers made their way back to the wagon train, carrying the girl and the Indian boy. Soon, Sky and Elizabeth were huddled under blankets next to a huge fire in front of the cook wagon.

Serena Hildebrand fussed over both of them like a mother hen, forcing hot broth from a steaming mug into their mouths, and kissing them both time after time. Christine sat on the cold ground next to Elizabeth, refusing to move or to let go of her sister. Danny and Dave huddled close by the girls. Behind them, most of the wagon travelers had gathered to celebrate Elizabeth's rescue and the end of the storm.

Scrapper John was nursing a cup of steaming hot chocolate when Wes Stone crouched next to him. "Seems to me you got some explainin' to do, John. You said you know this Indian? You sure he ain't one of that Sun Dog's men?"

Scrapper John stood, resting his hand on Sky's shoulder. "His name is Seeks The Far Sky. And yes, he rides with Sun Dog. Sky is my blood brother. He came here last night to warn me the train was gonna be attacked as soon as the storm let up. I asked him to take me to the Indian camp so I could reason with Tangled Face, to see if there was anythin' I could do to stop the Indians from attackin'."

"You went to their camp?" Stone growled with surprise. "You coulda been . . ."

"Darn right I went to their camp, Wes!" Scrapper John said. "I was tryin' to save your wagon train!"

"What did Sun Dog say?" Sweetwater Eddie asked.

"I didn't talk to him. Tangled Face said there wasn't no chance to avoid the attack." He hesitated for a moment. "The storm was hurtin' the Indians worse than it was hurtin' us 'cause we had food for a few days, an' the cattle, too. They got no food at all. I heard kids cryin' cause they was hungry an'—hey!"

He turned to Wes Stone. "I got a idea that jist might work. Suppose we offer maybe twenty head of cattle to Sun Dog to feed his people? Could be that would stop him from attackin'."

"The boy's got a right good idea," a man from the crowd said, stepping forward.

"He sure does!" another settler cried.

"We can't give in to them now!" Stone exclaimed. "If they're as bad off as John says . . ."

"This boy saved my life," Elizabeth called out from between chattering teeth. "Doesn't that mean anything?"

Dave Hildebrand stood up behind his daughter. "Darn right it does, honey," he said. He looked Wes Stone in the eye. "I supported you, Wes—an' I was wrong. Billy an' Scrapper John an' Eddie were right all the time, but I was too pigheaded to see the truth. But I can see it now." He faced the crowd. "I think Scrapper John's idea is a right good one. But I got another that jist might work. How about askin' if we can buy some land with our cattle? We don't know nothin' 'bout this area—an' even if our deed for Skull Mountain is good, it's still sacred to the Indians. There could be land jist as good a few miles off, an' maybe the Indians wouldn't mind us bein' on it."

"No!" Wes Stone snapped. "We ain't . . ."

Stone's protests were quickly drowned out by voices from the crowd.

"Good idea, Dave!" the big man named Vince said, stepping up to Dave Hildebrand.

"All we got to do is find Sun Dog an' make our offer . . ." Dave began.

"No need to find him," Sweetwater Eddie said, pointing to the east. A line of mounted Indians stretched over the hill, their horses standing hock-deep in snow. "Looks like Sun Dog an' his warriors has found us!"

Scrapper John stood. "Let me talk to Tangled Face and Sun Dog," he said. "Maybe I'm wrong, but I think Tangled Face jist may be able to convince Sun Dog to make a deal."

There was a long silence as Wes Stone stared at the crowd of settlers, anger written across his face. Then he turned and stormed off. Handing his mug to Serena Hildebrand, Scrapper John walked between two wagons, and began trudging through the snow toward the line of Indians.

Two days later, melting snow had turned the prairie into a sea of mud. The sun was warm, and the sky blue. The oxen and horses pulling the long line of wagons struggled to pull their burdens through the slippery mess. Tangled Face, with Seeks The Far Sky at his side, rode ahead of the first wagon. Another band of Indian warriors rode in front of them. Sun Dog sat on his horse off to the side, his rifle cradled in his arms.

Tangled Face drew rein and held up an arm. Dave Hildebrand and the wagon drivers stopped their animals. Riding beside the wagon train, Scrapper John and Sweetwater Eddie halted their horses, and waited. The Indian warrior turned his horse to face the settlers.

"If you were to go straight here, your blood would stain the land around what we call Skull Mountain. But instead, you will turn toward the sun. In one half day you will come to a great valley. That land will be yours forever, because you have bought and paid for it."

Scrapper John nudged Black Lightning up to where Sky sat on his own Appaloosa. The boys grinned at each other for a moment.

"You gonna stay with Sun Dog?" Scrapper John asked.

Sky held his hand out to his friend. "I will ride with Sun Dog for a while longer," he said. "But what happened here has convinced me that there is a better path than fighting."

The boys shook hands, still smiling.

Tangled Face pointed to the two boys, and called out in a loud voice, addressing the settlers and his warriors. "Let us watch these boys and learn from them," he said clearly, his voice ringing across the prairie. "Men like Sun Dog and Wes Stone have years of hatred weighing down their hearts. But these boys are friends and brothers. Your leader would take Sun Dog's life, and Sun Dog would take Wes Stone's life. But Scrapper John and Seeks The Far Sky would *give* their lives for each other."

Tangled Face paused for a long moment to let his words sink in. The only sound was the snorting of the animals and the whisper of a warm breeze.

"Who do you think is right?" he asked, facing first the settlers on the wagon train and then his warriors. Then he walked his horse to one side. The first wagon began a long turn, away from the direction of Skull Mountain and toward the valley where the settlers would make their home.

Scrapper John reined Black Lightning back to Sweetwater Eddie, who rode next to the Hildebrands' wagon. Scrapper John grinned at the mountain man. "We never did run that race we talked 'bout the day you come to fetch me to go to the Rendezvous with you."

Sweetwater Eddie patted his gut. "You might not have a chance, boy," he growled. "If Serena makes anymore of that cobbler of hers, I'll be too heavy for Zinger to carry." He rubbed his stomach again and belched loud enough to startle the Hildebrands' pulling horses.

Elizabeth peeked out the back flap. She smiled at Scrapper John and looked over at Sweetwater Eddie.

"Think it'll rain, Eddie?" she asked mischievously. "I think I just heard thunder! And don't you two go wandering off. My ma's got a special meal planned for tonight!"

Scrapper John winked at her. "We was just about to have a little race to see whose horse is faster," he told her. He slowed Black Lightning so that the horse lagged behind Sweetwater Eddie's horse, doubled his reins in one hand, and slapped Zinger's flank with them.

Feeling the lash of the mountain boy's reins, Zinger charged forward at full speed, almost jerking Eddie from his saddle.

"Why you little rascal, you . . . !" Sweetwater Eddie shouted, grabbing at his reins as his horse took off across the muddy prairie. "I'll get you for this . . ." he cried, his voice fading as Zinger galloped into the distance.

Scrapper John whooped loudly and urged Black Lightning forward. Quickly Sweetwater Eddie and Scrapper John were riding neck and neck across the wide open prairie, the two friends and their horses outlined against the bright spring sun and the mighty peaks of the great western mountains.

Celebrating 40 Years of Cleary Kids!

CAMELOT presents
CLEARY FAVORITES!

☐ **HENRY HUGGINS**
70912-0 ($3.50 US/$4.25 Can)

☐ **HENRY AND BEEZUS**
70914-7 ($3.50 US/$4.25 Can)

☐ **HENRY AND THE CLUBHOUSE**
70915-5 ($3.50 US/$4.25 Can)

☐ **ELLEN TEBBITS**
70913-9 ($3.50 US/$4.25 Can)

☐ **HENRY AND RIBSY**
70917-1 ($3.50 US/$4.25 Can)

☐ **BEEZUS AND RAMONA**
70918-X ($3.50 US/$4.25 Can)

☐ **RAMONA AND HER FATHER**
70916-3 ($3.50 US/$4.25 Can)

☐ **MITCH AND AMY**
70925-2 ($3.50 US/$4.25 Can)

☐ **RUNAWAY RALPH**
70953-8 ($3.50 US/$4.25 Can)

☐ **HENRY AND THE PAPER ROUTE**
70921-X ($3.50 US/$4.25 Can)

☐ **RAMONA AND HER MOTHER**
70952-X ($3.50 US/$4.25 Can)

☐ **OTIS SPOFFORD**
70919-8 ($3.50 US/$4.25 Can)

☐ **THE MOUSE AND THE MOTORCYCLE**
70924-4 ($3.50 US/$4.25 Can)

☐ **SOCKS**
70926-0 ($3.50 US/$4.25 Can)

☐ **EMILY'S RUNAWAY IMAGINATION**
70923-6 ($3.50 US/$4.25 Can)

☐ **MUGGIE MAGGIE**
71087-0 ($3.50 US/$4.25 Can)

☐ **RAMONA THE PEST**
70954-6 ($3.50 US/$4.25 Can)

A CAST OF CHARACTERS
TO DELIGHT THE HEARTS
OF READERS!

BUNNICULA   51094-4/$2.95 U.S./$3.50 CAN.
James and Deborah Howe, illustrated by Alan Daniel
The now-famous story of the vampire bunny, this ALA
Notable Book begins the light-hearted story of the small
rabbit the Monroe family find in a shoebox at a Dracula
film. He looks like any ordinary bunny to Harold the dog.
But Chester, a well-read and observant cat, is suspicious
of the newcomer, whose teeth strangely resemble
fangs...

HOWLIDAY INN   69294-5/$3.50 U.S./$3.95 CAN.
James Howe, illustrated by Lynn Munsinger
The continued "tail" of Chester the cat and Harold the dog
as they spend their summer vacation at the foreboding
Chateau Bow-Wow, a kennel run by a mad scientist!

THE CELERY STALKS 69054-3/$2.95 U.S./$3.50 CAN.
AT MIDNIGHT
James Howe, illustrated by Leslie Morrill
Bunnicula is back and on the loose in this third hilarious
novel featuring Chester the cat, Harold the dog, and the
famous vampire bunny.

NIGHTY-NIGHTMARE   70490-0/$3.50 U.S./$3.95 CAN.
James Howe, illustrated by Leslie Morrill
Join Chester the cat, Harold the dog, and Howie the other
family dog as they hear the tale of how Bunnicula was
born while they are on an overnight camping trip full of
surprises!